DRACULA'S BRIDE

IMMORTAL MONSTERS BOOK ONE

REBEKAH R. GANIERE

FALLEN ANGEL PRESS

ISBN: 978-1-63300-042-1
ISBN: 978-1-63300-044-5

Cover art by Rebekah R. Ganiere

DEDICATION

For those who embrace the Darkness

NEWSLETTER

To claim your Two FREE Books and find out more about Rebekah R. Ganiere and her other Upcoming Releases
You can Go Here:
www.RebekahGaniere.com/Newsletter

CHAPTER ONE

The Count gazed across the darkened sky across the window of his upstairs study. Piercing screams floated up the stairs, ruining the serenity of the otherwise plentiful moon. He raised a goblet to his lips and swallowed down the sweet, rich wine, allowing the taste of cinnamon and fresh berries to linger on his tongue. Melancholy settled inside him and, with it, the knowledge that this would be the last time, for quite some time, that he would stand at this window and gaze out at his beloved Romania. The last time he would take in the rich scents of pipe tobacco and polished wood from his cherished home. The last time he would be able to bathe in his solitude unhindered by prying eyes and wagging tongues.

"My Lord." Renfield knocked on the door. "We've... found her."

As if the Count hadn't witnessed the carriage arrive and Renfield jumping from the Coachman's seat to open the door for Kush, who'd struggled with the wild-haired woman in the bloodstained night-gown. As if he couldn't hear her yowls and curses as Kuch dragged her down the corridors toward the back of the castle. As if he hadn't caught the stench of death the moment the front door had swung wide, announcing her reluctant return.

"Was she spotted?" he finally asked.

"Yes."

Damn. He sipped his wine and looked to the woods. A pack of giant wolves emerged from the trees and stared at his window. He stared at the alpha for a minute, and then the animal bowed and returned to the darkness.

"How many dead?"

"Two children and a nanny."

His gut clenched. Children. Of anyone she could have harmed, a child was worst of all.

Her screeches and wailing faded down the lower hall, and the mechanisms inside the castle churned and creaked as a secret passage opened far below them.

He'd warned her. Death wasn't necessary, and children were a line they did not cross. Yet, even for all of his precautions, she'd escaped the house and done the worst thing imaginable. He was to blame for the deaths. He should never have taken her in the first place. But the ache that had left a hole in his heart for the past five hundred years had made him reckless, desperate even. But no more. It was time to take care of his mistakes once and for all.

"Was she recognized?"

"I'm... not sure, My Lord."

The Count turned to Renfield. "But it's possible."

Renfield bowed his head. "Yes, My Lord."

The Count finished his wine and set the goblet on the nearby table. He slowly unbuttoned his azure silk smoking jacket as Renfield rushed forward to help him out of it. Renfield hung it over his arm as the Count removed his cufflinks and handed them to his butler.

"Take her to the solarium and chain her. Then, pack everything. It's time for us to take an extended vacation."

He rolled up his sleeves one at a time and then walked to a spacious mahogany wardrobe. He removed a gold chain from around his neck and produced a hefty brass key.

"Write to Mr. Harker. Let him know that we will be arriving post-haste and to have the house ready. I wish to be gone before dawn."

The Count turned the key in the lock until the heavy metal gears scraped open and the doors popped apart.

"Of course, My Lord, but..."

He stopped and turned.

Renfield shifted from foot to foot. "Should we plan for everyone to go?"

The Count pushed the doors apart, gazing over the dozens of items inside the bureau. Knives of all shapes and sizes. Crossbows. Guns. Stakes. Swords. Crosses. Holy water. Garlic oil. Bolts. Arrows. Pistols. Axes. If man had made a weapon, he owned one.

Reaching into the cabinet, he pulled a blue, velvet-lined box from its spot on a small shelf. His hand hovered over the box for a moment before opening the lid. He stared at the thin silver dagger set with his family crest and red rubies. Blowing out a breath, he removed it from its resting place. Weighing the weapon, he allowed the silver to sear into his palm. Pain washed up his arm, across his shoulder, and down his side, as his skin reddened, blistered, and then blackened. He fought the urge to recoil from the weapon as his fangs lengthened, and his body cried out for relief.

He deserved the torture. He deserved the reminder of what he was responsible for and guilty of. He closed the cabinet doors. He deserved to make penance.

The Count turned at Renfield. It would be so much easier to leave by himself. Head to England and start fresh. To rid himself of his mistakes and begin again. But this problem was of his own making. He had lain in his bed; now, it was his job to make it.

"Yes. We all go." He headed for the door and stopped as he passed Renfield. "All but one."

MINA CARRIED THE DELICATE TUREEN OF STEW OUT OF the stuffy kitchen and into the fading dining room. Though her father hadn't once invited guests over in the last two years, he still insisted on having a formal dinner every night.

"It's about time." Her oldest brother, Arthur, put his cigarette out in the ashtray.

"What is it?" asked Quincey.

"Stew." She set the chipped china in the middle of the once grand table, which was in sore need of refinishing.

"Ugh, again," complained Lucy. "I can't swallow another spoonful of Mina's miscellaneous vegetable stew."

Mina's cheeks heated, and she bit back the words she wanted to yell at her spoiled, selfish siblings.

"Father, can I get you some?" Mina reached for his bowl.

He looked up from his paper and smiled. "Thank you, Mina."

She set the tureen on the table and stepped back as her brothers ladled out two huge portions. Lucy went last, taking a ladleful and dropping it into her bowl. She sniffed the stew and looked up at Mina.

"What's in it this time, anyway?"

"We still have some potatoes, and I tried to rehydrate the dried chipped beef. There are a few carrots and—"

Lucy pushed the bowl away. "Never mind. I'll just have bread."

Mina swallowed hard. "There isn't any."

"What?" her brothers said in unison.

"There's no flour left. I have to go to town tomorrow and get some."

"Did you hear that, Father?" said Arthur. "We don't even have any flour left."

Their father turned the page of the paper, still ignoring them.

"Well, what is left?" demanded Quincey.

Mina looked at the stew bowl.

"We'll starve," Lucy cried. "There's no way I can live off stew for the rest of my life."

"Well, why don't you find someone to marry, and then we'll have one less mouth to feed?" said Arthur.

"We who?" Lucy retorted. "If you two would get jobs, we could afford some food."

"You are just as capable as we are," retorted Quincey. "I don't see you out trying to get a job as a housemaid or a shop girl."

Lucy jumped to her feet. "I'm not suited to work like that. You know I have a weak constitution."

"Weak constitution, my ass. You're nothing more than a lazy socialite past her prime."

Lucy gasped.

Their father's hand slammed on the table, cracking through the argument and making the bowls shake.

"Enough!" he shouted. You will eat, thank Mina for keeping you from having to feed yourselves, and stop complaining."

The siblings looked at each other and then, in turn, mumbled their thanks to Mina.

Arthur stabbed at his stew and grumbled to himself. "Knew those ships were a stupid investment."

Their father slowly lowered his paper. "What did you say?"

The blood drained from Mina's body as she backed toward the wall.

Arthur and Quincey looked at their father while Lucy stepped away from the table and turned her fearful gaze toward Mina.

"Don't you move." Father pointed at Lucy. "You are just as ungrateful. Your younger sister has been the only one of you with an ounce of empathy for me and what I've been through!" He slammed his fist on the table again, making everyone jump.

"Father, I didn't mean any disrespect," Arthur said.

"Didn't mean disrespect? Didn't mean disrespect?" He leaped from his chair and rounded the table quicker than Lucy could get out of the way. He grabbed Arthur by his silk ascot and yanked him to his feet, knocking him into Lucy. "You, Quincey, and Lucy. I let your mother spoil you in my absence. So lazy that you don't even have the skills to secure a job. I should have thrown you and your brother into the Navy. Made you men instead of the pandering dandy boys you've become. Squandering the little inheritance you got from your grandfather on gambling. Forcing me to sell half our land just to keep feeding your fat bellies, and you don't even have the decency to marry the girl I arranged for you, saying she wasn't pretty enough. And now you have the gall to dare and tell me how to run my business? Say it again."

Mina took half a step forward, trying to decide if she should intervene, but Lucy caught her eye and shook her head. She'd seen this anger in her father before.

In the past year, since losing his money on a bad investment tip about some ships bringing goods from China, she'd seen that look in his eye more frequently, and each time, it had scared her less and less. She wondered why that was. Suppose she'd just become so conditioned to the violence that it no longer seemed out of place. Though he'd never once raised his hand to her, she wondered if she'd still not be scared if his anger was ever aimed her way.

"I... I don't have anything to say," Arthur stammered.

"Are you sure? Because you seemed like you had

something to say to me. Quincey, didn't he seem like he had something he wanted to say?"

Quincey didn't reply.

Father looked at Quincey. "Oh, now you don't have anything to say?"

"No, sir," Quincey replied.

Father pulled Arthur closer.

"I'm... I'm sorry, Father. I didn't mean—"

His fist smashed into Arthur's stomach, doubling him over. Lucy cried out and scrambled out of the way. Their father elbowed Arthur on the back, making him buckle to his knees. Mina watched, partly fascinated, partly stuck in her spot, as always.

He kicked Arthur in the face, sending him sprawling backward. The dining room chair tipped over as Arthur went down and hit the wooden floor with a *thwack*, again making Lucy cringe like a whipped puppy. Mina couldn't understand how Lucy, who could be as cunning as a panther when it came to men and as backbiting as a viper when it came to gossip, could be so squeamish when it came to physical violence.

Blood poured from Arthur's nose and the corner of his mouth, down his silk shirt, staining it. Father kicked him in the stomach again, and Mina stepped forward. If she didn't step in, Arthur was liable to not get up off the dining room floor alive. She stepped over her brother and wrapped a dishtowel around her father's hand.

She gave him a gentle smile and dabbed at his swelling knuckles. "I'll make a soak for your hand."

He breathed heavily, his wild gaze scouring her face. Mina continued to dab his knuckles, keeping her face passive. Minutes ticked by in tense silence, except for Arthur's gurgling wheezes. Finally, her father's eyes softened, and regret filled his features, though he'd never apologize.

The doorbell rang, and everyone turned toward it. A moment passed, and then the bell rang again.

"I'll... I'll get it." Lucy struggled to her feet and headed for the door.

"No. Mina will get it," her father said. "Quincey, help Arthur to his room... and get him a drink."

Lucy stopped in her tracks and nodded.

Mina pushed through the dining room door to the front hall. She walked to the entrance and stopped. She checked her clothing for blood, brushed her hair over her shoulders, and pinched her cheeks. Planting the best smile she could muster, she pulled the door open.

In front of her stood a tall young man with bright red hair and a smattering of freckles across his nose. He clutched a simple bouquet of wildflowers. Mina recognized them as the ones that grew between her house and the vast estate next door, which he was being paid to care for.

"Evening, Ms. Murray."

"Mr. Harker."

He held the flowers out further to her, and she took them like she had a million times before.

"Jonathan, you need to stop picking flowers from the estate. They aren't yours to take."

He shrugged. "Come on, Mina, it's no big deal." He threw her a broad smile and patted down his unruly hair. "May I come in?"

Mina's gut clenched. "Not tonight. Father isn't feeling well."

"I'm sorry to hear that. Well, can you come out for a moment? I want to ask you something."

Mina tried not to chuckle. "Are you going to ask me to marry you again?"

He licked his lips. "Maybe."

"Jonathan, I've told you every time you've asked me since we were ten I love you as a brother and nothing more."

"Ahhhh... But when we were six, you said yes, you would marry me. So I'm not giving up."

Mina shook her head and smiled. Jonathan was sweet, and if she was honest, she liked him a lot more than either of her brothers, but she loved him only as a friend, and she didn't see that changing.

"What could be better than marrying your best friend?" he asked.

It had been the same argument every time she'd refused. For all of Jonathan's great attributes, having dreams wasn't one of them. He didn't understand that she didn't want to marry her best friend. She wanted passion. A love so all-consuming that her body would freeze without the warmth of her husband next to her. She wanted adventure and to see the world.

"Jonathan—"

He held up his hands. "It's fine. I understand, but I'm not giving up."

She shook her head and sighed. "I wish you would go into town and take wildflowers to one of the other girls. Fanny Coventry has always fancied you."

"Fanny Coventry fancies anything on two legs that isn't already taken."

Mina tried not to laugh, but the statement was true. The girl flitted from one true love to another.

"Besides, within the next few days, I fear I won't have time to court anyone."

"Did something happen?"

"The Count sent word yesterday. He's finally arriving. Honestly, I thought I might never get to meet my employer after all these years of working for him."

"So that's why you proposed again? You don't think you have time to find someone else?"

"Of course not. It's just that I've been working for days to prepare the estate for him. We still have so much to do to prepare, and I have no idea when I will be free again to have time for myself."

"So you'd marry me and leave me to fend for myself while you always work?"

"Mina—"

She stepped out the door and squeezed his arm. "I'm kidding, Jonathan, breathe."

He huffed. "Why do you tease me so?"

"Because you make it so easy."

"Andromina?" her father called from down the hallway.

Mina's smile dropped as fast as if someone had kidnapped it from her face. She stepped back through the doorway. "I have to go."

"Meet me tomorrow by the old oak. We can have lunch together. Charlie will be there."

She loved seeing Jonathan's little brother, Charlie. "I thought you were too busy to do anything? Besides, I must go into town and get food to stock the pantry."

Jonathan's expression saddened, and he stepped up and kissed her cheek. "If you married me, I would care for you, Mina. You wouldn't have to go to the store and buy on credit, mend your brothers' clothes, or take your sister's ruined hand-me-down dresses. I would give you the world."

It was true. Jonathan would be a good provider monetarily, but emotionally and mentally, she wouldn't be challenged. As much as she adored him, she couldn't see trying to converse with him about much more than what they talked about now. The estate. Her family. His little brother refused to attend school and skipped in the woods behind her father's estate. His mother's gout and what the weather might be like in the next year. Jonathan was comforting company but not all that stimulating.

"Andromina."

"I must go. Good luck with your employer. I know he will find you to be a fine caretaker."

Mina closed the door and looked down at the flowers. Every time Jonathan came, it was the same. Four blue flowers, three yellow, six white. And if she married him, that would also be her life. Predictable, monotonous, dull.

Mina walked down the hall and stopped by a vase filled with his last withered bouquet. She changed out the flowers and continued back toward the dining room. Dropping the dead flowers in a wastebasket, she entered the now-empty dining room. She needed to make a soak for her father's hand and scrub Arthur's blood out of the floor before it set. Heaven knew they couldn't afford to buy more cleaning supplies than necessary.

An hour later, Mina sat on her heels, her spine crying out from having been bent over so long, and surveyed her work. She dipped her hands into the bucket and then wiped them on her apron, staining it pink. She stared at the wooden floor. Her father's eagle eye would notice even a speck of blood.

"It's good enough."

Mina looked up to find Quincey smoking a

cigarette in the doorway. She grabbed onto a chair for support and pulled herself to her feet. She reached for the bucket, but Quincey stepped forward.

"Let me." He bent and took it for her, swaying slightly as he did.

Wonderful. He'd been drinking again. Quincey was nothing if not predictable. Every time Father got physical, Quincey got scared and drank. Mina stared at him momentarily, and her guard raised like the drawbridge on a castle. Quincey never did anything unless there was something in it for himself.

"Thank you." She walked with him through the dining room and down the adjoining corridor. The small servant's passage smelled of moldy wood, and they'd long since stopped filling the gas wall sconces, leaving the confined space to feel eerily small.

When they reached the kitchen, Mina blew out a breath she didn't realize she'd been holding. Quincey shuffled to the back door, opened it, and threw out the water before returning the bucket to the corner.

Mina cleaned up the scraps of this and that, ensuring everything was ready for her to make breakfast in the morning, all while keeping her eyes on Quincey.

"So, Jonathan was at the door?"

A niggling of anticipation trickled up her spine.

Quincey leaned against the wall and puffed his cigarette. "Did he ask you to marry him again?"

She brushed carrot peels into her palm and walked them to the waste bin.

"He did."

She caught Quincey staring at her out of the corner of her eye. Sick of dancing around the subject with him, she faced him.

"What is it you want to say to me, Quincey?"

He snuffed out his cigarette on the cracked plaster behind him and pitched the remainder into the trash.

"Why do you not marry him? Don't you know what his income could do for our family?"

So that was it. Money. How had she not seen that coming?

"Jonathan's income is his alone. I would not burden him with a wife who brings an extra four mouths that need feeding. Especially ones as ungrateful as you lot."

Without warning, Quincey lunged toward her but miscalculated and slammed into the counter as Mina grabbed a knife from the butcher block.

"I wouldn't do that," she warned. "I told you last time that I'd never let you lay a hand on me again. In case you forgot."

Quincey looked at the knife and licked his lips. A crooked smile turned up the corners of his mouth. "You don't have it in you to stab me."

Mina straightened her shoulders. "Don't mistake my demur nature for one of weakness, Brother. I've seen enough blood-soaked floors and walls in this house to know when to hold my tongue and when to fight for my life. I've not been pushed that far yet, but that doesn't mean I couldn't be."

Her heartbeat pounded, and she fought to keep her hand from shaking as she squared off against Quincey. He stood stock-still for a moment and then chuckled and stumbled backward.

He pulled a cigarette from the case in his pocket and lit it. "You surprise me, little sister. I thought that all the Murray spit had gone to Lucy. I see now that I may have been wrong in that assessment."

"Andromina?" Her father's voice floated down the hall. "It's time to shut up the house."

Her eyes never left Quincey. "Coming, Father."

Her heart continued to pound as Quincey finally turned and walked out of the kitchen.

Mina stood, arm outstretched until she was sure he'd left, and then she crumpled to the floor, the knife clattering to the ground. Tears stung her eyes, and she sucked in a ragged breath before she swiped at her face and sniffled hard. She'd learned years ago that weakness was liable to get you hurt in this family, so she'd taught herself to lock hers away, never to be seen.

But just like the dilapidated walls that surrounded her, Mina knew, sooner or later—with enough weight —everything crumbled to dust.

She looked up at the ceiling and took in a shuddered breath. Two brothers, one sister, and a father.

Four other people to share a house with. Four people to share a life with. And yet... she could rely on no one but herself.

She had to get out of her father's house. She wasn't sure she would make it out alive if she didn't.

CHAPTER TWO

Arthur winced as he hitched the horse to their carriage. Mina bit her tongue against the offer of help that sat upon it. To do so would only gain her a much-unwanted tongue-lashing at the very least. After her run-in with Quincey the night before, she wasn't sure what either of her brothers were capable of anymore.

She stood on the stoop and waited for him to finish. Behind her, a giggle sounded, and Lucy rushed down the stairs, her robin's egg colored dress fitting her curvy figure perfectly. Her honey-blonde hair was expertly coiffed and set beneath her bonnet.

Mina looked down at the faded green frock that she'd taken in for her more slender form after Lucy had finished with it. It paled in comparison to her sister's outfit but then everything Mina was paled in comparison. It no longer made her jealous; it had merely become a part of her life.

"Are you done?" Lucy called to Arthur.

"You can do it yourself if you want it done faster," Arthur yelled.

Lucy linked her arm with Mina's in a way she'd not done in years.

"I am so excited to get out of the house," she whispered. "I am much in need of conversation and fresh air. If I have to spend one more minute smelling Quincey's horrible cigarette smoke, I might just choke and die."

Mina smiled blandly and watched Arthur finish with the horse. He turned to them and held out the reins.

Lucy squealed and ran to the carriage. She held out her hand to Arthur.

"What?"

She rolled her eyes. "Help me up."

He slapped the reins into her palm. "Help yourself."

He headed back toward the house. Mina stepped in his way, and he looked at her and clenched his jaw. His left eye was swollen shut, and the entire area puffed like a bloated, dead fish.

"I have a few aspirins left in the top drawer of my desk. You may have them if you wish."

"I'm fine." He brushed past her, and Mina sighed and shook her head.

Lucy called out, and Mina headed toward the carriage.

Lucy climbed in the back as Mina took the reins and settled on the coachman's bench. Mina sat holding the reins for a moment, regretting asking Lucy to come along. She should have been used to being treated like a servant, but even so, it still stung.

Finally, Mina slapped the reins, making the horse trot down the drive toward the road.

MINA DIRECTED THE HORSE TOWARD TOWN, AND THE closer they got, the faster and more incessant Lucy's talking became. She talked about clothing, ribbons, parties, friends, and on and on. Mina silently watched the trees go by until the houses grew closer together and the traffic heavier. She wove through the other carriages and stopped in front of the store.

She slid to the ground as Lucy exited the back like royalty.

Mina patted the horse. "Good boy, Doc." She pulled two sugar cubes from her pocket and held her hand out to the horse.

Lucy grabbed her wrist. "You told me there was no more sugar a week ago."

Mina ripped her hand away. "These are mine. I saved them from my tea."

She held her hand out to the horse again, and his soft lips nuzzled her palm as Lucy huffed beside her.

"You should have shared those with us instead of wasting them on the dumb animal."

Mina's temper flared. "Did you pull us to town?"

Lucy pursed her lips and turned away.

"I didn't think so." Mina pet the horse's ears and then walked into the shop with Lucy.

Mina pulled her list from her pocket as she walked around checking prices. Lucy went straight to the bolts of fabric and ribbons and began ogling them at length.

"Good morning, Miss Andromina," said Mr. Giles from behind the counter.

"Good morning, sir. How are you today?"

"Better than last week. Is there anything I can help you get today?"

"Yes." She smiled and handed him her list.

Mr. Giles looked it over and added it up. Her heartbeat quickened as the numbers rose beyond what they could afford.

He handed the paper back to her, and she stared at the sum. "Will that be cash today?"

"Uhm... I... I was hoping we could maybe—"

He squeezed her hand and gave her a broad smile that lit up his cherubic face. "Let me look in my ledger and see what I can do."

She nodded in gratitude.

Mr. Giles bent under the counter and pulled out a worn leather-bound book. He flipped through the pages, then stopped and ran his finger down a column. His brow furrowed, and Mina swallowed hard.

"Well." He scratched his head. "I might be able to do a little, but I'm afraid it's been quite a while since your father has made a payment." He looked at her sympathetically.

Mina swallowed the lump in her throat and turned to see Lucy tying a ribbon in her hair.

Mina looked down at the gold bracelet hanging on her wrist. Her chest squeezed hard, and she slipped it off.

"Do... Do you think that this might... Could you possibly..."

Mr. Giles took the bracelet and looked it over. He licked his lips and nodded. "I believe we could come to an arrangement. A piece like this could cover most of the debt as well as whatever you get today."

"Thank you." Her voice cracked.

Lucy waltzed up and dropped a handful of ribbons on the counter. She smiled at Mr. Giles and looked at Mina's bracelet.

"Isn't that the bracelet that—"

"Yes," Mina whispered.

Mr. Giles looked between them. "I'm afraid this payment won't cover the ribbons."

Lucy smiled. "That's not a problem. I'll pay for them." She opened her purse, pulled out a few coins, and set them on the counter.

"You have money?" Mina fought to keep the surprise from her voice.

Lucy looked at her out of the corner of her eye and shrugged. "You had sugar."

Mr. Giles's expression hardened, and he slid the money back to Lucy and pulled the ribbons away from her.

"I'm afraid I can't sell you those ribbons."

Lucy's brows furrowed. "Why not? Is this not enough?"

He looked to Mina and then back to Lucy. "I'm afraid those ribbons are spoken for. I forgot."

"Well, then I'll just grab a few others—"

"They are all spoken for."

Lucy's cheeks reddened, and she snatched her money from the counter and shoved it in her purse. "How dare you not offer me service. My father—"

"Your father, I am sure, would be most happy to hear that you have saved some money for yourself. Perhaps you would like to put it toward his bill of goods that he uses to fill your stomach with."

The pink in Lucy's cheeks deepened.

"Is there a problem?"

Mina turned with Lucy to see two well-dressed young women standing by the door.

"Octavia! Sera!" Lucy screeched. She ran to her friends and threw her arms around them.

"Lucy, how are you, my dear? We haven't seen you in ages."

"We've been so busy at the house," she said. "Father is always entertaining. But today, I just had to come get some new ribbons. It seems, however, that Mr. Giles is all out of the quality I am looking for."

Octavia linked her arm to Lucy's. "Well then, we shall go to Mr. Berkdorm's across the street. He has the most beautiful silk ribbons in right now."

"Yes." Sera took Lucy's other arm. "Then we shall all go to Aunt Gladys' for tea."

"That will be most lovely." Lucy and her friends walked to the door. She stopped as they exited and looked over her shoulder at Mina. "When you've finished shopping, you can join us at Berkdorm's."

Mina watched as the three trotted across the street to the other store. For a moment, she wished that she, too, had friends to giggle and gossip with, but then she remembered she neither giggled nor enjoyed gossip, so what would be the point?

Mina turned to Mr. Giles. "Do you mind packing up the carriage with my things?"

He nodded. "Not at all, my dear. And here." He pushed the bracelet back toward her. "I can't take it."

She shook her head. "No. I won't have you continuing to carry our debt."

He looked at the bracelet and then put it in his apron pocket. "A loan then. I'll keep the bracelet as collateral. Just as soon as your father can pay me back, it's yours."

Mina smiled. "I am most grateful."

He shooed her away. "Go now. Go see what Berkdorm's offers that is better than my little shop."

She squeezed his hand. "All the goods in the world are worthless compared to the kindness of friends."

He chuckled. "And for that, my dear, I give you a gift." He opened a jar of peppermint candies and spooned several into a small paper bag.

"I can't—"

"You will. And I will be glad to see you with them."

"You really are too kind." Mina took the peppermints and walked out of the store. She stepped onto the busy sidewalk and could swear that even from where she stood, she could hear her sister laughing and giggling with her friends.

Head down, and thoughts on what had transpired in the shop, Mina stepped into the street barely conscious of anything around her. Someone to her left shouted. She looked up in time to see a shiny midnight-colored carriage with two muscular black steeds bearing down on her. Mina froze on the spot as the horses headed for her. Like a fog rolling across the moors, her vision fuzzed over, and she swayed. Her mind told her to move, but her body refused to budge. She couldn't look away, as if something inside called to her soul.

Time slowed to a crawl as the horse's hoofbeats thundered in time with her heart. All around her, people screamed and waved for her to move, but Mina's gaze stayed fixed on the elegant, inky carriage.

Suddenly, a pair of strong arms pulled her out of the way. Mina caught her breath as the carriage passed by so close that it blew the hair from her face. The carriage pulled to a stop just beyond where she stood, and the driver looked back at her.

"Are you all right, Miss?" the man who'd saved her asked.

Mina looked at him and then back at the carriage. "Yes. I'm fine, thank you."

A second carriage followed the first. The driver of the second carriage yelled to the driver of the first carriage in a language that sounded similar to Russian. The primary driver motioned to her and said something she didn't understand. The curtain to the second carriage pulled aside a crack, revealing a black-gloved hand. Mina's heart raced as she tried to see into the depths of the murky carriage. The second driver hopped from his seat and rushed to her.

"Are you all right, Madame?" His thick accent rang with a sensual quality. "The horses are not used to the cities yet." He tucked his long white hair behind his protruding ears.

Mina tittered. "Then you shouldn't take them to London."

He gave a tight smile, revealing slightly crooked teeth. He glanced at the second carriage for a moment and then nodded slightly. "My master sincerely apologies for any discomfort you may have been subjected to."

His master?

"Tell your employer I am just fine."

The man looked to the second carriage, and the gloved hand stayed put for a moment and then disappeared from view.

"Again, my most sincere apologies, Madame."

"Mina. I'm just Mina."

"Of course, Lady Mina."

"No... Your apology is accepted. Think nothing more of it."

The man hurried back into his seat, yelled at the first driver, and the carriages moved forward at a slower pace.

Mina watched them roll on, unable to remove her gaze. In the shadow of the second carriage, she felt an undeniable pull as if the carriage itself beckoned to her. The black rear curtain moved inches to the side, and from deep within, a pair of bright blue eyes peered out at her, making her suck in a breath. Everything around her faded away as she and the owner of the blue eyes continued to stare at each other. She found herself following the carriage as if the person beckoned her forward.

Suddenly, a tug on her arm slammed Mina back into the present as Lucy, Octavia, and Sera stood at her side. She wanted to slap her sister for stopping her, but as she caught the gazes of several towns-people staring at her, she held back her impulse. Sounds and smells bombarded her as she tried to get her bearings. It was like she'd been in a dream and awakened violently.

"Do you know who that was?"

"Did he say anything to you?"

Mina could barely process their words as the blue eyes still pierced her thoughts. "I... I don't know—"

"The man in the carriage," said Octavia. "Did you see him?"

The women looked at her expectantly.

"No," said Mina. "Who?"

"That," Sera said, "is the man who bought the estate right next to yours. Count Draugr."

"I hear he's loaded." Octavia smirked. "Houses all over Europe and America."

"I hear he's gorgeous." Sera swooned, making Mina roll her eyes.

"Well, I hear he's going to be the man I marry," said Lucy.

All three laughed and linked arms again before heading down the sidewalk.

Mina watched the black carriages disappear. That was the new Count.

"Are you coming?" called Lucy. "Or are you going to just stand in the street with your mouth open?"

Mina took one last look down the street, then walked to the sidewalk and followed the gaggle of women toward Aunt Gladys' house for tea, trying to understand what had just happened to her.

CHAPTER THREE

Blue stepped out of the carriage as Renfield held out a parasol to shade him from the sun's blinding rays. He blinked rapidly and shielded his eyes even though clouds marred the sun's penetrating gaze. He hurried toward the front door of his new estate, and Renfield opened the door for him just as his blood heated, burning him from the inside out. Blue hurried through the door and almost ran over a bright-haired young man with wide, innocent eyes. He fought to keep his composure as pain seared every particle of his body, like liquid lightning in his veins.

His mind continued to drift to the striking girl from the village. She'd focused on him like she could see through the light-blocking curtains.

"Mr. Jonathan Harker?" Blue questioned.

"Yes, your Lordship."

Blue continued forward into the safety of the house, forcing Jonathan to step back into the foyer. Shakily, Blue removed his gloves and hat and handed them to Renfield. He looked Jonathan up and down, his fangs aching for sustenance to heal the boiling inside him.

"You're younger than I expected." He walked to the nearest table and ran his finger down it in an appearance of checking for dust.

"I... I promise my age does not reflect my work ethic," Jonathan stammered.

Blue looked back at him for a moment and then nodded. "I hope that is true."

He stepped through the foyer and looked up at the grand staircase that wound both to the right and the left. In the center of the open landing hung an enormous portrait of Blue himself. The painting was the only piece of his belongings he carried from estate to estate when he moved. Everything else remained where it was. The painting had been sent on ahead of his arrival, and it satisfied him that someone had shown initiative in unpacking it and placing it in such an appropriate spot.

He wanted nothing more than to go upstairs to his new room and collapse into bed. But he held back in an effort to show some conventionality to his new staff, though he was sure he wouldn't be keeping many of them now that he'd arrived.

Blue strode to the left and opened a set of ornate

double doors. A parlor had been arranged for entertaining. It's not that Blue intended to do much of
that, but it at least gave the appearance of normalcy.
The salon led into a gentleman's smoking room and
study. Blue walked from room to room, slowly
admiring the English craftsmanship of the deep wood
paneling. He inspected the study, wandering to the far
side of the room and glancing out the heavily
curtained window before striding to the mantle and
scanning it.

The massive wooden piece stared at him, regal
and elegant. He ran his fingers over the tops of the
design, which included two intricately carved camellia
flowers.

"So this is it?" he asked Renfield in his native
tongue.

Renfield stepped forward and nodded. *"It is."*

Blue looked up to the ceiling and then listened to
the sounds of the house. Within the room, he could
barely hear the whisper of the winds howling outside,
even with his enhanced hearing. He looked at the fireplace again. It would suffice.

*"I would like all of the servants lined up in the front hall
so that I might meet them."*

Renfield nodded and left the room.

As the burn inside him subsided, Blue took a
moment to breathe deep. The journey had been long
and exhausting. Weeks of riding in the carriage.
Then, the sea voyage. Back to the carriage again.

He'd never felt so trapped before. His thoughts turned to the beautiful girl from earlier.

"Mr. Harker?" Blue called.

Jonathan walked in. "Your lordship?"

"In the village today. There was a girl. Raven-haired, pale skin, intense, emerald, doe-like eyes. Might you know her?"

"It's possible that could be Miss Mina Murray. She is the Admiral's youngest daughter. They live next door, sir."

Blue nodded. Mina. Such an interesting name for such an exotic girl. "She was with a blonde girl, bright clothing, the giggly sort."

Jonathan nodded. "That was definitely Mina and her sister Lucy."

"Do you know them well?"

Blue did not miss Jonathan's affectionate smile. "Since we were children. Mina and I are to be married."

Blue couldn't help the look of surprise that he knew overtook his features. "Is that so?"

"Well..." Jonathan shifted from foot to foot. "When she says yes, we will."

"So you have not proposed?"

"I've proposed. She is just... unsure as of yet."

Blue nodded, understanding all too well the boy's affection for the beauty. He'd felt her before seeing her —a pull in his gut that had forced him to move the curtain and look out the window despite the danger the sun posed to him. And to be met by such a mesmerizing face... sharp, wide-set eyes. Small pixie nose. Deep crimson lips just begging to be kissed. All set upon a face, a shade too pale and high cheekbones sunken in just enough to give the appearance that she didn't eat as much as she should.

Standing there in the street, right in the path of his carriages, as if she sensed him as well. She'd stuck to the spot, and for a fraction of a moment, he'd feared they might run over the beautiful creature, but Renfield had gotten hold of the horse just in time to miss trampling her. And more so to save Blue from having to fly from the coach and save her, exposing himself to everyone in this new town as his skin would have begun to char. But it would have been worth it to protect someone as striking as she.

"Is something wrong, sir?" Jonathan's question pulled Blue from his memory.

"No. Only I wanted to apologize again for almost trampling her in town today. Perhaps you can get her something in the village if you know what she likes. I will then send it over with a note."

A troubled look crossed Jonathan's face, and then he bowed. "Of course, my Lord."

He left as Renfield entered and stared at Blue, a scowl on his wrinkled old parchment face.

"You have something to say?"

Renfield opened his mouth, closed it, and opened it again. "Only that we have just arrived, sir. Perhaps looking for a companion might wait a bit, all things considered."

Blue's anger brewed and churned, causing his vision to redden slightly. He breathed deep and turned away from Renfield, knowing his old friend meant only to help.

"Until nightfall, the coffins are to remain locked and inside the carriage. Ensure Kush takes the carriage to the stable and locks it in."

Renfield nodded. "Will do, sir."

"As soon as it is dark, and Mr. Harker and the other servants have gone home for the night, you, Iona, and I will deal with them."

"Very well, sir."

"And Renfield?"

The man turned back.

"Make sure to have Kush set a slab of raw meat out in the woods for my friends. They've had a long journey as well."

Renfield nodded before exiting.

Blue turned to the window, careful not to let the light touch his exposed skin. Beyond the house stood acres and acres of green gardens and open space to run. And beyond that lay acres and acres of forest that separated his property from the next. Blue's budding happiness gave way to hope, but he quickly quieted the sensation. He didn't want to have to move again. Didn't want to have to run in the night again. Didn't want to have to burn a woman alive and then behead her again. To avoid those things, he would need to be smarter this time. He would need to be more resolved this time.

He would need to stay away from his next-door neighbor, Mina Murray.

MINA ENDURED THE TEA WITH HER SISTER AND HER friends and thanked the heavens that it only lasted part of the afternoon. She couldn't help but let her mind drift to the blue eyes that stared at her from the darkness of the carriage. But with the memory came a flood of questions.

How could she possibly have seen eyes like that in such total darkness? Had she imagined them? A flight of fancy perhaps—not that she'd ever been prone to that.

Lucy parted with her friends, and Mina gathered their wagon and headed home.

"You could have been nicer, you know," Lucy called from her throne in the back.

Mina kept her eyes on the road. "I don't know what you mean. I was perfectly pleasant."

"Pleasant, yes. You are always pleasant, that is true. I didn't say you weren't pleasant. I said you weren't nice."

"And what do you consider nice?"

"Speaking. Laughing. Offering conversation."

She nodded. "Interesting. You consider talking about the weather and gossiping about the women we know being nice."

Lucy clucked her tongue and huffed. "And this is why you will never marry a man of wealth. You just do not understand what is expected of society women."

"Who said I wanted to marry a rich man? When I marry, it will be for love whether he has as much money as the king or as little as we do."

Lucy sighed and shook her head. "Well, then, better for me. I intend to marry the richest man I can find. Bearing him a couple of sons and then spending as much of his fortune as I'm able."

"Yes, well, you always have cared more about things than people."

Lucy didn't see the insult, which was fine with Mina. The tedium of the day had begun to grate on her nerves.

They rode the rest of the way in silence. Along the way, Mina spotted Charlie running down the road after a quick little rabbit. He laughed and waved and kept going.

Lucy jumped from the coach when they reached home, leaving Mina to deal with the horse. Her brothers walked out and looked through the boxes of supplies.

"No cigarettes?"

Mina rolled her eyes. "No money."

Quincey took the reins to the horse as Arthur pulled the crates from the carriage and carried them inside.

"Did everything go all right in town?"

Mina gave him a tight smile and nodded.

"No hassle from Mr. Giles about credit?"

"Nothing I couldn't handle."

Quincey's brow furrowed. "Handle how?"

Mina shrugged. "I gave him collateral for the bill."

"What do you have that you could give as collateral?"

A pit deepened in her stomach. She moved around her brother, and he caught her wrist. She stared back at him, and he lifted her wrist, looking at it.

"Mina, you didn't-"

She pulled away. "Food is more important than trinkets."

"That wasn't a trinket."

"And Mr. Giles will keep it for me until I can repurchase it."

She headed toward the front door.

"Jonathan stopped by and dropped something off for you."

Mina groaned inwardly. When would he learn? She headed up the steps and stopped by the table at the front door. A small box sat on top with a beautifully scrawled envelope. It wasn't Jonathan's handwriting, and the box looked much more expensive than anything Jonathan would consider purchasing.

She opened the envelope.

My Dear Miss Mina,

I apologize for the mishap in the village today with our carriages. I hope you will accept this small token and apology and that we will meet in person soon so I can apologize again.

Yours Most Sincerely,

Count B. Draugr

Mina read the note three times before putting it down and picking up the deep crimson box. Her heartbeat kicked up even before seeing what the box held. She opened it and gasped. Inside sat a golden hair comb encrusted with little jewels. Mina ran her fingers over it, fascinated. The light blue gemstones reminded her of the blue eyes she'd seen in the coach.

"Andromina?"

She turned at the sound of her father saying her name.

He looked her up and down, strode forward, and picked up the envelope. She stood perfectly still as he took the box from her and looked inside. His gaze shifted to hers.

"What happened?"

Mina swallowed. "It was nothing. His horses got away from his driver and charged toward me."

"Were you hurt?"

"Nothing but my pride. Lucy was there with her

friends. I can never do anything right when it comes to Lucy."

He stroked her hair, and his heavy hand fell on her shoulder. "I shall go have a chat with our new neighbor. Teach his servant to keep better control of his animals."

"No, Father," she blurted. Her mind moved quickly, and she smiled, trying to cover the blunder. "I simply mean that I don't want to be an even further embarrassment to you."

His eyes softened. "Of all my children, you are the only one who doesn't embarrass me."

For a moment, she saw the father she'd heard stories about from her siblings. The one who had been gentler and kinder. The one who had laughed and joked and thrown parties. The father from before the death of the mother she'd never known. Dying only a month after Mina's birth, the loss had changed him forever, she'd been told.

Like a puff of smoke, the softness left his face. "Very well. I will not say anything this time. But there will be a reckoning if you have another unfortunate encounter with this Lord or his manservant."

Mina lifted on her toes and kissed her father's cheek. "Thank you."

He glanced down at the box. "The comb is too much, though. Even for my most precious child. It shall go back."

Mina knew better than to let her disappointment show. "Of course."

Though she had no inclination for fancy things, knowing that the comb might have come from the person inside that carriage made her want to wear it.

Her father returned the box to her and then strode into his study. Mina clutched the comb tightly. If she took the thing straight to her room and locked it away, would her father even remember she'd been given it in the morning? She looked down again. It was pretty beautiful—something that looked like it'd come straight out of her mother's old jewelry box. Before, they'd been forced to sell everything to pay the bills.

Mina tucked the box into her hands and turned for the stairs. She got two feet before she stopped. She was being silly. Why should she be having that kind of reaction to someone she'd never seen nor met before? She was not that person—materialistic, vain, secretive. She shook the nonsense from her head and set the box on the table. She refused to be as light-minded as her sister.

MINA BRUSHED HER LONG DARK HAIR BEFORE HER vanity mirror and stared at her reflection. She analyzed her face as she'd done dozens of times before. Her nose was smaller than Lucy's, but Lucy's round, brown eyes were much more proportionate to her face. Mina felt her cheekbones were her best feature, although Lucy had told her they were too pronounced and made her look gaunt. She didn't exactly dislike her porcelain skin, though. The contrast of her dark hair made her lips take on a deep hue that even Lucy and her friends envied.

All in all, she called herself average. Not beautiful like Lucy with her honeyed hair and peachy complexion, but not as bad as to be considered ugly either. Aside from Jonathan, she'd never had a suitor, but she assumed that was due more to her father's stern demeanor and reclusive nature than her looks.

Was she doing herself a disservice by rejecting Jonathan's offer of marriage? Surely, living as his wife would be better than staying in the house she now lived in.

Marrying Jonathan would bring what? Stability? Yes. Loyalty? Yes. Happiness? Perhaps. But it would also bring her brothers, with their hands out, Lucy always making snide little comments about everything and days full of longing. And if she was honest with herself, she cared about Jonathan too much as a friend to saddle him with a wife who would not be content as he would.

After setting her brush down next to her comb and small hand mirror, she stood in her thin chemise and pulled the sheets down on her bed. She thought about climbing in, but her gaze traveled to the window. She wondered if she looked out, if she would be able to see the candles lit at Count Draugr's estate.

She'd played every B. man's name she could think of through her head in the previous hours. Bryson, Branson, Bert, Bryan, Brandon, Blain, Bob, Billy, Braden, Blake, Bernie, none of them seemed to fit the man that had been described to her over tea as the most handsome and exotic man ever to grace England—though none of the women at tea had ever laid eyes on him.

Curiosity pulled her to her balcony. Opening the doors, the sheer curtains billowed outward, calling her forward. The brisk wind whipped her recently brushed hair to and fro. She stepped into the night and walked to the edge of the terrace. Looking out at the land surrounding her father's house, she wondered how long the solicitors would wait before they auctioned everything off and took the little that remained.

Acres of green surrounded by a thick forest. A dense fog rolled across the expanse like a blanket of dirty cotton. She stared as far as she could, and up on the hill, barely bigger than an apple, sat Count B. Draugr's estate. She couldn't tell whether the lamps were lit from that distance, but something told her they were.

She speculated what he was doing that late at night, staring at the structure until the fog covered it in its chilly grip, protecting the abode from her prying gaze. Mina shivered at the ominous sight.

Movement near the edge of the property caught her attention, and she squinted and tried to focus on it. Her heart leaped as she made out the outline of an imposing black dog prowling through the fog toward the house. It kept to the edge of the property, skirting the perimeter of the family cemetery. Behind the first, several other black dogs emerged from the trees and waited.

Mina held her breath, watching the animals. As her eyesight adjusted to the moonlight night, she realized they weren't dogs. They were wolves. But... There were no wolves in England. She'd never even seen a live wolf before. She'd read about them and seen photos, but wolves hadn't been in England for hundreds of years.

The lead wolf stopped at the garden's edge and stared at her. Mina regarded the beautiful creature, struck by how the moon glimmered off its blue-black fur. Her fingers twitched, wanting to run through his coat to see if it was soft or coarse. She was about to turn from the balcony and go down when a shot rang through the air. The wolf flinched, and Mina looked over her balcony. Her father stood below with his rifle pointed at the animal. She opened her mouth to yell and tell him to stop when the wolf glanced up at her and then raced off toward the trees. Her father trained his rifle on the wolf again, and Mina held her breath.

He shot once more as the wolf's form faded into the darkness. He stood momentarily longer, turned, and headed into the house. Mina's heart pounded. A wolf on their property. But where had it come from? And what was it doing there? And most of all, why had it been staring at her?

Mina kept her eyes on the tree line for a quarter of an hour, hoping the wolf would reemerge, but there was no more sign of him. She prayed that her father hadn't hit him, but somehow, she knew he hadn't, and the thought soothed her.

CHAPTER FOUR

Blue stood in the shadow of the forest, watching Mina on her balcony. Her beautiful loose-hanging hair and ivory chemise whipped around her as she wrapped her arms tightly around herself. Despite Renfield's warning, he couldn't help but want to be near her. Unlike all the others, his body yearned for her. It wasn't the same this time, he convinced himself. She was different. She'd not screamed at the sight of him in wolf form. Not run or even flinched. She'd stared at him, watching him. Intent. Curious even. Traits he'd not expected to find in an English woman. However, it had been close to a hundred years since he'd visited England, so things might have changed.

He needed to be careful, though; her father owned demons that Blue had seen all too many times. He had smelled the alcohol on the man from yards away, and the man had swayed as he'd tried to level his gun. The pain in the man's deep brown eyes had also spoken volumes. Blue knew that pain intimately and the fury that accompanied it. He wondered if Mina had ever been a victim of her father's anger. He prayed she hadn't.

Blue waited an hour or more before once again heading toward the house. He'd sent the rest of the wolves off to patrol the area and made his way alone across the fog-laden garden.

All lights had gone out in the house, and his hearing picked up nothing more than the sounds of hearts beating slowly and breathing deep and even. His two natures battled as he convinced himself to turn around and go home, leave the girl in peace, and focus on fitting in and setting up his house.

But in the end, he couldn't bring himself to turn away. Not with her balcony doors still open and his ability to sneak in unencumbered. All he wanted was one look. Just one look up close at her face to see if she was the beauty he'd thought or if he'd imagined it. Then, he would leave her be. Beauty or not. Drawn to her or not. He would let her go for her good, as well as his own.

He kept to the shadows until he was directly under her veranda. He shifted from wolf form into humanoid and walked to the wall. His nails lengthened, and he jammed his fingers into the sides of the stone. Quick as lightning, he climbed to her balcony and dropped down onto it soundlessly.

He caught her scent of peonies and mint from where he stood. Moving cautiously toward the billowing curtains, he didn't know what she'd do if she awoke to find a man standing in her bedroom—or what her father would do. Even so, he had to chance it.

Blue pushed through the sheer fabric and stepped into a once opulent room faded by time and, presumably, a lack of funds to maintain it. The wallpaper, which had once been brighter, now sported little more than a drab gray tinge. The vanity in the corner sagged on tattered legs. The wardrobe, too, had seen its share of years, as one door had lost its handle and the other hung loosely on its hinges.

Mina's influence permeated every aspect of the room, from the timeworn wallpaper to the corner filled with a spider web-lined cradle and ratty dolls.

A comfortable-looking bed with a thin white bedspread and sheets sat in the middle of the space. Her ebony hair fanned out over her pillow, her skin as pale as the sheets surrounding her. Blue stepped closer. It had been so long since he'd been with a woman. His fangs ached, and his throat burned to taste her. Just a simple taste to sate the thirst that had built inside him over the weeks of travel. A sip to savor and carry him through. To make his soul's desire abate and allow him to carry on with what he needed to focus on.

The vein at her throat pulsed deep purple against her skin. Blue swallowed hard, but it did no good. Her blood whispered to him like a terrible dream. He wanted to look away. Move away. But he couldn't. She lay peaceful and serene before him as if the gods had made her just for him. Blissfully unaware of the danger he presented.

Mesmerized, he stood at the head of her bed, watching the rise and fall of her chest. The rhythm of her breathing lulled him into wanting to lie next to her and hold her. What about her drew him in the way she did, without having ever met her? He had no idea, but he couldn't deny the seduction of her soul against his. Had his heart still beat, indeed, it would have mimicked the rhythm of her own. She'd not spoken a word to him, and still, Blue couldn't control the feelings building inside him. She was meant to be his.

He moved closer, his body almost touching hers. He brushed a strand of hair from her warm skin and bent closer. One kiss. That was all he needed, and then he would be satisfied. One kiss. One taste. One bite. He brought his lips down to hers, barely caressing her warm flesh. Her soft breath caught on his tongue, and he pulled away in a flash. What was he doing?

The sudden movement made her eyes flutter

open. She looked at him with sleep-drenched eyes, and then her gaze sharpened.

In an instant, Blue blended into the deepest corner of her room. She sat up and stared at him as if she saw him standing there. Clutching her sheet, she again didn't look afraid, only confused. She stared right at where he stood.

It wasn't proper for him to be in her room like this. She deserved better. Blue needed to go.

He drifted into the night in a puff of smoke and shadow, his thirst forcing him toward town.

He needed to feed.

BLUE RUSHED TOWARD LONDON. HIS FANGS BURNED, and his throat ached with the need for sustenance. He reminded himself of the rules he'd set forth two hundred years prior as he landed on the cobblestone street and melted into the shadows. No children. No elderly. No sick. No addicted. Women were only an option if they were willing.

He stalked the streets, moving like smoke on the wind between the towering brick buildings billowing noxious soot into the sky. Deeper and deeper, he headed into where the buildings leaned closer together as if trying to lend each other support. He knew he was headed in the right direction when the smothering aroma of filth and decay bombarded him as he crept through the tightly packed buildings strewn with laundry drying overhead and babies screaming from hunger. The scent of people packed in tighter than a slaughteryard overwhelmed him. So many bodies. So many pleasures. So much blood.

He pressed against a cold stone building as Mina's face flashed into view. Hair fanned out. Face pale and innocent. Body slender and ripe. He fought the instincts growing inside him that wanted to fly right back through her window and make her his.

The sound of shuffling feet and giggling pulled his attention. He pushed deeper into the shadows as a wiry man and an ample-breasted woman staggered around the corner. The man draped his arm over the woman's shoulders, forcing her to support most of his weight as he swayed in the dimly lit alley.

"Come on, love, let's get you to bed," she crooned.

He shoved her off, and she bumped into a wall. "I told you, I don't want a bed." He leaned against her body and pressed her into the wall, kissing her. "You know what I want." He ran his hand down her bosom to her waist and then kissed her neck as he fumbled to lift her skirt.

She pushed at his hands, keeping a smile on her face. "Come on, you know I don't do that anymore. I'm respectable now. I simply wanted to ensure you got home safe because I am fond of you."

The punch came out of nowhere, leaving the woman no time to react. The crunch of bone reverberated through Blue's ears as the man's fist connected with the side of her cheek, and the woman went down like a discarded rag doll. The drunkard poised over her, still swaying.

"Now, let me show you how fond I am of you too, Betsy Boo." He grabbed the waistband of his pants and began to undo them; the woman didn't even stir as she lay unconscious on the ground.

Rage crawled over Blue, sharpening his vision and spiking his hunger. Blue was on the man in a flash. Shoving him into the shadows, Blue didn't even try to be gentle. He ripped at the man's throat, tearing the flesh and causing as much pain as possible. Thick blood hit his tongue, gushing into his mouth. He gulped down the fresh sustenance, barely even taking notice of the man's feeble attempts to beat at his back. Blue slammed the man into the brick, hitting the man's head with a crack. Warm liquid flowed through Blue's muscles, strengthening him and bringing him a euphoria that few other things in his long life could achieve.

The drunk man's limbs slackened, and Blue had to hold him up to keep him from falling. The man's heartbeat slowed, and his breathing labored... labored... and stopped. He took one final draw and then looked into the man's eyes. They focused on Blue for half a second before the light within dimmed and went out. Blue stared at him for a moment, trying to muster even an ounce of remorse for killing the man. He couldn't.

MINA AWOKE THE FOLLOWING DAY TO WORRY, threading through her bones, though she couldn't pinpoint precisely why. She started toward the kitchen to prepare breakfast as a knock sounded on the side door.

"Good morning." Jonathan grinned at her from the doorstep.

Mina forced a smile. "Jonathan, what are you doing here? It's early."

"I've been up all night, and I'm just now going home."

"What kept you?"

"My employer. He sure is a strange one."

Her stomach clenched. "He just got here."

"He just informed the staff that he expects us to keep new hours. He no longer wants us there by five and home by nine. Instead, he intends for us to not start until noon and stay until three in the morning. Some nights even later."

Mina fought the urge to ask Jonathan if the Count had blue eyes, what he was like, and any number of other silly questions her sister would have asked while she gossiped with her friends.

"But you know that long hours are required. You've all been lucky you've had several years where you didn't have to work that long with the Count being away. That had to end at some point," she offered. "If you don't like it, you can always threaten to quit."

"I have a feeling the Count doesn't take threats lightly. If I even tried, he'd probably dismiss me." Jonathan shook his head. "I've not met a more sullen and peculiar man all my life."

"Maybe he just isn't used to our customs. Perhaps where he comes from, they keep a different schedule."

Jonathan nodded. "Perhaps. Not that I would dare ask. He went on a walk last night around ten and didn't return home until after two. Didn't say a word to me as we passed in the hall. He simply went up to his room and shut the door."

Had he been in the forest between their lands? Had he seen the black wolf, too?

"I should get going. I need to sleep before I am to return." He turned to go and then stopped. "By the way, did you get the package he sent?"

"Yes. Which reminds me, I should give it to you to return for me."

Jonathan studied her for a moment. "Your father won't let you keep it."

She shook her head. "It's much too nice anyway. Wait here. I'll be right back."

Mina walked into the front hall and retrieved the small box. For a moment, she was tempted again to defy her father and keep it, but she knew better. Unlike with her siblings, he'd never raised so much as a finger against her, but tempting the devil was to invite him in.

She handed the box to Jonathan. "Please tell Count Draugr I thank him for the gift and accept his apology."

A slight smile played across Jonathan's face as he looked at the box.

"What?"

He looked up. "Nothing. I just... nothing. I'll try to stop by later if I'm able."

She nodded, and he headed down the walkway.

"Jonathan?"

He turned.

"What does the B stand for in Count Draugr's name?"

"Blue, I believe, or at least that's what he says his friends call him. I cannot imagine him having friends with how few words he speaks and the stern gaze he gives everyone."

Mina nodded. "Oh, and one last thing. Tell Charlie to be careful; I think I saw some wolves in the woods last night."

Jonathan shook his head and chuckled. "There are no wolves in England. Probably just a pack of hunting dogs on the loose. But I'll tell him to be careful nonetheless."

Mina closed the door. Blue... she wondered if it was for the blue eyes she'd seen in the carriage.

. . .

THE DAY LANGUISHED IN TENTATIVE SILENCE. MINA'S father left mid-morning to try to secure financing for another flotilla of trading vessels, and her sister and brothers spent their day in their bedrooms, leaving Mina to her books and her thoughts. Around lunch, she checked on Arthur, finding his wounds healing. Then, she went to the kitchen and set out what she needed for dinner before returning to her room.

Sitting on her bed, she found her gaze turning toward the corner of her room. The corner where she could have sworn she'd seen a man standing the night before. A man who had disappeared into the shadows and then floated out into the night in a puff of smoke. She knew it was most likely a silly trick of her mind, but still, she couldn't get past how real it had seemed.

She walked to the French doors and opened them before stepping out onto her balcony. She again looked across her father's land to the estate next door and wondered what the mysterious Count Draugr was really like. In the distance, she caught Jonathan's bright red hair as he trekked up the green with Charlie's light, shaggy head skipping along next to him. Frees-spirited Charlie was so different from Jonathan, who took his duties as seriously as he had taken his schooling when they were younger. Despite their considerable age difference, the two were as close as two brothers could be.

Though Jonathan hadn't said anything complimentary toward the Count, Mina wondered how much of what Jonathan had said was because he envied the man, much like how she envied Jonathan for a moment. He got to work for and see the Count. A position she would have loved to obtain. To see how he'd changed the estate since the last time she'd visited her childhood friend Gretchen. It'd been many years, but she still remembered it as if it had been her own home.

The sound of carriage wheels crunching up the drive pulled Mina's attention. Horses cantered toward the house, pulling Octavia's flamboyant carriage. Mina watched with mixed emotions as her sister's best friend jumped from the coach and dashed for the door, leaving her driver sitting in his place. Mina couldn't remember the last time Octavia had come to visit. Mina wondered if seeing the girl for the second time in two days had something to do with Mina's new neighbor. She looked toward the house on the hill once more in time to see Jonathan disappear inside.

MINA REACHED THE LANDING TO FIND OCTAVIA already deep in conversation with Lucy. She descended the staircase, and Octavia stopped abruptly. Lucy turned, spotted Mina, and then linked her arm to Octavia's and ushered her into the drawing room. Mina shook her head and headed to offer the driver something to drink. He graciously accepted and followed her into the kitchen, where they sat and talked about horses and the weather for the better part of an hour.

Finally, Lucy marched into the kitchen, grinning like a cat with a mouse in its mouth.

"Octavia is ready to go home."

The driver nodded and stood. "Thank you for your kindness, Lady Mina."

Mina flushed. "It's just Mina. And you are welcome any time, Robert."

She sipped the rest of her tea, picked up the cups, and placed them in the sink. She'd started washing the dishes when Lucy returned from her goodbyes and lingered beside Mina, arms folded, still grinning. Her sister's energy grated on Mina instead of making her want to know what Lucy had to say. When Lucy was ready, she'd vomit up the most recent gossip. And just like the previous million times Lucy had been bursting to tell Mina the news, Mina didn't care one whit.

"Aren't you even going to ask why Octavia was here?" she finally cried.

Mina fought the rolling of her eyes. "I assumed it was to see you."

"Don't be such a twit. She was here to tell me about the morning paper. There were two murders in London last night. Two."

Mina shrugged. "People die every day."

"Yes, but these two men were found with their throats slashed to ribbons and drained of blood."

Mina stopped scrubbing the tea saucer but didn't look up. No blood? That was different. "Did they find out who did it?"

"More like, *what* did it. Some say it was wild animals, and others say a crazed lunatic."

"Well, it's good that London is nearly fifty miles from us then. We don't have to worry about anything like that happening here."

"Even so," said Lucy. "We should ensure the house is locked up extra tight in the evenings. You never know who or what is lurking around outside anymore."

Mina's thoughts went to the giant wolf she'd seen on the grounds. Surely wolves couldn't run fifty miles in a night and kill people, could they?

"Do you want to go for a walk today?" Lucy asked suddenly.

Mina couldn't remember the last time Lucy had asked her to do anything.

A twinkle settled in Lucy's eyes.

Mina fought to keep a nonchalant expression on her face. "What are you up to?"

Her sister shrugged. "I just thought maybe we could go on a walk. Possibly up to Count Draugr's estate."

The way Lucy refused to meet Mina's eye told her

Lucy had something particular in mind- and simply going for a walk wasn't it.

Even so, Mina couldn't deny that she also wanted to visit the adjoining estate. Something about its eerie, looming presence drew her to it like never before. And she was dying to see if the eyes she'd seen the day before belonged to the Count.

"Just let me finish a few things, and we can go after lunch."

Lucy threw her a giant grin. "Great. That will be enough time for me to get ready."

Lucy flounced out of the kitchen, and Mina stared after her. She was tempted to call out and tell Lucy she wasn't going after all. Not because she didn't want to, she most desperately did, but because the look in her sister's eyes had given Mina the feeling that what-ever Lucy was up to, she was sure not to like it much.

CHAPTER FIVE

Mina waited until almost a quarter of three before her sister finally made an appearance. She could barely hold in her surprise at seeing Lucy wearing her nicest daytime frock and hat as she sauntered down the stairs. A pair of white gloves adorned her hands, and she'd rouged her cheeks and lips.

"You do know we are just going for a walk, not to a tea party," said Mina.

Lucy gave a nervous laugh. "Oh, sister, I want to ensure I look my best. In case we run into anyone interesting."

Mina furrowed her brow.

Lucy refused to meet Mina's eye as she bustled to the door. "Shall we go?"

Mina regarded her sister as she opened the door and headed out.

"Where are you two going?" Quincey descended the stairs.

"For a walk," Lucy announced. "And if we aren't back in time, you'll have to fend for yourselves for dinner."

"Walk, dear sister? I thought you hated walking. Preferred to be carried around on a golden chair like Sheba."

Lucy made a face at Quincey and then stormed back inside, grabbed Mina's hand, and dragged her out the door.

"Ignore the ignorant," Lucy called over her shoulder as she slammed the front door.

Lucy stomped down the driveway. Mina followed, shaking her head. Lucy made everything a spectacle. She couldn't even go for a simple walk without putting on a show.

THEY WALKED IN SILENCE FOR A GOOD TEN MINUTES before Mina finally spoke.

"You haven't wanted me to walk with you in ages, and when we walk, we usually go into the woods or through the gardens, not out on the open road."

"I just... felt like it was such a lovely day that I couldn't bear to be cooped up one minute more. Don't you get tired of being inside? Cooking. Cleaning. Listening to Quincey and Arthur complain and play cards?"

Of course, she got tired of it. She also got tired of listening to her sister's complaints. And her father's drinking. Not that she would ever give voice to any of those things with Lucy.

"We would all do well to try and help out where we can. To try and better our circumstances and lighten the load."

Lucy snorted. "Oh, Mina. You are such a goodie-goodie."

"Whatever happened to Mitchell Wellesley? I thought you said a few months ago that you were sure he would propose."

Lucy wrinkled her nose. "Turns out I didn't like him as much as I thought."

Mina glanced sideways. All Lucy had done for weeks was gush over Mitchell, his money, his houses, and his horses. Then suddenly, one day, she'd just stopped.

Lucy looked at Mina. "All right, fine. Mitchell got drunk with Arthur and Quincey one night, and Quincey lost a substantial amount of money to him—money he didn't have and couldn't repay. Mitchell beat the tar out of Quincey, and I haven't heard from him since."

For a moment, Mina was tempted to feel bad for her sister. Their brothers were something Mina would never understand. They'd both been educated at a prestigious boarding school. They could have gone on to get high-paying jobs or to college because of who their maternal grandparents were. Instead, they'd banked on their inheritances and their father's money to get them through life... unfortunately, that hadn't turned out well for any of them. They'd already been forced to sell land for the last three years to keep afloat. It surprised her that her father hadn't forced them to go to London to look for work, but then that would let society know just how bad off they were.

"He's engaged to Melody Spencer now, I'm told," said Lucy. "But I don't care. I'll find someone better. As a matter of fact, I bet you anything this time next year, I'll be married and off on a vacation somewhere exotic."

They rounded the bend, and the stone wall that separated their property from the Count's stood mere feet away. In the overcast light, the estate looked much less portentous than the night before. No longer shrouded in fog, it appeared a lonely building, as drab as its uninteresting landscape.

Even from that distance, the once beautiful architecture had fallen into disrepair. Eaves drooped. One of the chimneys had dropped. The shutters were in dire need of a fresh coat of paint. Even the grass looked as though it had given up its will to live.

"What do you think he's like?" asked Lucy.

"Who?"

"The Count. I heard he's handsome with hair and a beard, so black it appears blue. And eyes so bright that they shine like the moon."

Mina glanced sideways at her sister. "Have you been reading the fantasy novels in the library again?"

"No. When she came over this morning, Octavia told me that her cousin Mary had a friend from school who knew the maid's daughter who used to work in the Count's house when he lived in Spain as a young man."

Mina shook her head. "Well then, I'm sure it's true."

Lucy huffed. "Why do you have to ruin everything?"

"Me? What did I do?"

"You—" Lucy's words cut short as she stumbled into a small divot in the road. She cried out as her ankle twisted, and she went down.

Mina fought the urge to laugh at seeing her sister on her rump, dust all over her skirt.

"Owww," Lucy mewled. "My ankle."

Mina shook her head and bent down to look. She touched her sister's ankle, and Lucy cried out in pain.

"I can't walk," moaned Lucy.

"I'm fairly sure you can."

Lucy picked up a handful of pebbles and threw them at Mina. "Can't you see I'm injured? You don't have a sympathetic bone in your body, just like Father."

The words slapped Mina like a wet towel to the face. Her father was a hard military man who'd lost his wife, his business, his livelihood. He was forced to live only on his Admiral's pension, which wasn't near enough to pay for the house and lifestyle he'd grown accustomed to. All while trying to keep up the appearance that everything was all right. It was enough to make any man crack. And because of that, Mina sympathized with him- even so, she had no inclination to be like him.

Mina looked around. "Well, I'm not carrying you, that's for sure."

"I need help." Lucy's gaze went to the Count's estate. "Go. Get someone to help me home. I can't possibly walk."

Mina stared at her for a moment. "You're serious?"

"Most serious. If I walk on it, I could injure it further. Possibly so bad that I might never walk again."

Mina had a sound mind to leave her sister and head home. But if she did... who knew what Father would do? She straightened and shook her head. She couldn't believe she was about to do it. Lifting her skirt, she slid over the stone wall and trudged up the grassy hill toward the Count's main house. She had to admit she wanted to see the Count with her own eyes but to call on him for such a silly reason was beyond embarrassing.

. . .

MINA TRUDGED TO THE FRONT DOOR OF THE imposing stone estate. Her assessment from the road had been correct; the house was looking worse for wear. She wondered if the Count intended to upgrade it a bit. And why had Jonathan never done anything about it? She banged on it using the massive dragon's head knocker that she didn't remember from when she was a child.

She waited a minute and then knocked again. Looking over her shoulder, she could just make out Lucy sitting on the wall. Mina shook her head. She was about to turn and leave when a set of crisp foot-steps clicked toward the door, and the lock turned. On the other side stood the short, white-haired man who had jumped from the carriage to help her a few days before.

"May I help you, Miss?"

"Uh... Hello, I'm Mina from next door. My sister and I were walking, and she fell and twisted her ankle. I wondered if I might borrow your wagon to bring her home. I'll return it post haste."

He peered over her shoulder.

"I know this is quite an imposition, but she says she cannot walk and—"

"I can do it." Jonathan appeared at the door. "I'll get Miss Mina and Miss Lucy home and then return before the Count arises."

The butler looked between them and nodded.

Jonathan moved around him and squeezed out the door.

"So Lucy fell?" He took her arm and led her toward the stable.

"So she says."

"You mean she didn't fall?"

"Oh, she fell. I doubt that she's hurt as badly as she claims. I just can't figure out why she is making such a fuss."

Jonathan glanced over at her. "Are you sure you aren't being a bit harsh?"

"Not in the slightest."

TEN MINUTES LATER, THEY RODE TO WHERE LUCY SAT on the wall, listening to Charlie talk about the animals he'd seen that day. She smiled when she saw them.

"Oh, Jonathan. Finally. Thank you so much for coming." She reached out for him as he jumped from the wagon.

"It's not a problem at all, Miss Lucy. I hope Charlie wasn't bothering you."

"I was keeping her company while she waited," said Charlie.

Jonathan nodded. "Why don't you head on home? I'm sure Mom has to be wondering where you are by now."

Charlie hesitated and looked up at Mina. "Bye, Mina. Mina Jelly Beana."

Mina smiled. "Bye, Charlie Parlie Googly Darling."

Charlie laughed. "That barely rhymes."

She nodded in agreement. "I'll work on it."

Lucy rolled her eyes. "Children."

Jonathan helped Lucy to her feet as Charlie ran off. "I'll get you in this wagon right quick, and we'll be off to your house where you can get comfortable."

Lucy dropped her arms. "My house?"

Jonathan looked between Lucy and Mina. "Yes. I mean, isn't that where you wanted to go?"

"Certainly not. I can't ride that far in the wagon with my ankle in pain. It's already swelling like a melon. Going to the Count's estate is a much better idea."

"Oh, Lucy, the Count doesn't like visitors..."

Suddenly, she swooned, and Jonathan caught her right before she fell off the wall. In an instant, it all became clear to Mina. Lucy hadn't wanted to go for a walk at all. She'd wanted an excuse to see the inside the Count's house.

Jonathan looked to Mina for help. "What do I do?"

Mina shook her head, and her gaze pulled toward the nearby estate. Something in the house called to her, and for a split second, she thought she caught a glimpse of bright blue eyes watching her from an upstairs window.

"I think we better take her to the Count's." Mina

shook her head. "Who knows what is wrong with her."

BLUE AWOKE TO A PRESENCE IN THE HOUSE THAT HE couldn't place. He rose from his bed and dressed quickly. Opening his bedroom door, he heard voices coming from his downstairs parlor. He strode from the corridor of his bedroom wing and down the first flight of stairs. The voices grew louder—two women, Renfield and Jonathan. He floated across the landing and stopped short at the scent that hit his nostrils. *Mina.*

He fought to keep from flying down the bottom staircase.

"If I give you a glass of water, will you get back in the wagon and go home?" asked Renfield.

"I told you," said a female. "I can't possibly move with my ankle this swollen."

Blue descended the stairs deliberately and headed across the foyer to the parlor. He stopped just out of sight and took a deep breath. He needed to slow down so as not to lose control. Planting a simple smile on, he entered the doorway and took in the scene.

A blonde-haired woman lay in the lounge, her foot on a pillow. Next to her stood Mina, still as a statue. She looked up at Blue as he entered, and their gazes met just as they had on the street. He contemplated how to approach. Friendly? Aloof? Irritated? He wasn't sure what was expected of him anymore in England by men of culture like himself.

As the moments ticked by, Mina continued to take him in, showing no indication that she had spotted him in her room the night before.

"Good evening," Blue finally said, with a slight bow. He looked at the blonde on the couch, who he assumed was her sister, Lucy. "What have we here?"

The blonde smiled brightly and batted her eyelashes. Jonathan turned with a worried expression chiseled onto his face. Renfield looked more annoyed than usual, but it was Mina that Blue couldn't keep his gaze from traveling to.

"My Lord, this is Miss Mina and her sister, Miss Lucy," said Jonathan. "Lucy twisted her ankle and then swooned when I went to take her home."

Lucy's simpering smile forced Blue's fists to clench. "Count Draugr, I am so sorry to impose upon you like this, but it seems I just couldn't make it all the way home on my own. Please forgive me."

Blue caught Mina's left eyebrow raise ever so slightly as she attended her sister. Interesting.

He smelled the lie on Lucy's lips, and apparently, Mina did as well.

"Of course." Blue gave another bow. "Renfield, please get our guests something to drink and perhaps two aspirin for Miss Lucy."

Renfield stared at him momentarily before Blue

turned his gaze on him heavily. The butler bowed and exited the room.

"Miss Mina," said Blue. "I would like to apologize once again for the recklessness of my driver and horses the other day."

Mina nodded. "No harm done."

Blue crossed to her and lifted her hand to his lips. "Still, I could never forgive myself if something had befallen you." He sniffed her hand before letting his lips touch her skin. His fangs ached to be let down, but he withheld.

"Yes," Lucy interjected. "We are so grateful that nothing happened to little Mina. She means so much to us."

Lucy reached out and pulled Mina away from him. He straightened, attempting not to let his annoyance show.

Mina's expression was not affectionate, but she let Lucy hold her hand for a moment anyway.

Renfield returned with a tray laden with several glasses of wine.

"Thank you, Renfield. I can take it from here." Blue took the tray from him and set it on the coffee table.

Again, Renfield shot him a leery expression but did as he was told. Blue turned toward Mina and Lucy, noting they no longer held hands.

Jonathan stood in the doorway, and Blue waved him off. "If I need you, I shall call Mr. Harker."

Jonathan's cheeks flushed, and he hesitated before bowing and exiting the room.

Blue handed Lucy a goblet of wine and two aspirin. She flashed him a broad smile as he dropped the medicine into her palm. He reached for the other two goblets and lifted one to Mina.

"No, thank you."

Again, interesting. Blue nodded and put the wine back on the tray.

"Just because Mina won't doesn't mean we can't," said Lucy.

"I'm good," replied Blue. "Now, let me look at that ankle of yours. I have some training with anatomy."

"Are you a physician?" asked Mina.

He looked up at her to find her beautiful eyes full of interest. "No, but I have studied the human body quite extensively."

She considered him for a moment like one would consider a small object they weren't sure they were ready to purchase. Blue wanted to engage her, to say something witty and make her laugh, but now was not the time. It was too soon.

He sat on the table next to the lounge and gently lifted Lucy's ankle.

"It's so swollen. I'm afraid I may never dance again."

"That would be a pity." And a total lie. Her ankle was no more swollen than his.

"Do you dance?" asked Lucy.

"I have been known to dance before. Perhaps once your ankle is better, I shall throw a party and invite every one of note to attend. We could have a ball at the same time."

Not that he wanted anyone in his home. He'd be more than happy to keep to himself. But he'd learned long ago that the best way to keep people from looking too closely at your peculiarities was to show them you were just like them. And that meant showing them his home.

"Oh, that would be lovely. I know everyone, so if you need help finalizing a list, I would be more than happy to come over." Lucy batted her eyelashes.

"That's not necessary. I would hate to take you from... whatever you have to do."

She laid her hand on his forearm. "It would be my pleasure."

Blue fought the urge to laugh at her attempts at flirting. They did nothing to stir him except to make him wonder if her flatteries worked on other men.

"Would you attend as well, Miss Mina?"

He couldn't help but catch the anger that had planted on Mina's face. Her expression pacified immediately at the mention of her name, and she inclined her head.

"If you should wish it, I would come."

He couldn't help but smile. "Then it is settled. I shall send out invitations for this weekend."

"So soon?" said Lucy. "But there is so much to do."

"Oh, don't worry. I'm sure that I can pull it off. Besides, it isn't about the show. It's about the company." His eyes lingered on Mina, and a beautiful peach blush crept up her cheeks.

FOR THE NEXT HALF HOUR, BLUE CHATTED WITH Lucy. Mina chimed in only occasionally when he pointed questions right at her. It took him less than ten minutes to sense the dynamic between Mina and Lucy. Where Mina was sweet and quiet, Lucy could make or break his proposition of a relationship with Mina. One word of dislike to Mina or their family could spell disaster for him. He'd take Lucy's incessant chatter and giggles if it meant he could spend more time with Mina. But at some point, he wished to get her alone. Gossiping about those in their circle wasn't something he preferred to waste eternity doing. He wished to talk about more stimulating things, and those things he was sure would come from Mina, not Lucy.

As Lucy explained to Blue why the Devonshire family was not up to receiving an invitation, Mina suddenly rose from her seat.

"We should be going."

Lucy frowned. "But it isn't even sundown."

"I am sure Count Draugr will want supper soon, as will Papa, Arthur, and Quincey."

"Well... I mean, I could eat, now that I think of it." Lucy gave Blue an innocent smile.

"Great," replied Mina. "Then I shall get Jonathan to take us home."

Before Blue could protest, Mina strode from the room and headed toward the back of the estate. He couldn't help but love her pluck. It showed that although she allowed Lucy to take the lead, Mina refused to be pushed around.

"Mina!" Lucy called. "How rude! You can't just go running through other people's houses."

Blue smiled. "It's all right. You stay here. I'll go find her."

"I am so sorry."

Blue bowed and headed in the direction Mina had gone. He breathed in her scent and flitted down the hallway toward the kitchen, where she marched like she'd done it dozens of times.

She'd stopped by the kitchen door and set her hands on her hips before blowing out a harsh breath. She mumbled something he couldn't hear, but he got the feeling it was about her sister.

He stopped at her back and breathed in the rose water perfume of her hair. He fought back a groan at her sweet scent and the burn of his fangs as they pushed against his gums.

She spun around, eyes wide, but she neither

gasped nor screamed. Fascinating. He'd not met a woman like her before. Most women he'd met in England were pearl-clutching, naive Puritans.

His thoughts turned to her father, and again, he wondered if the man had ever hurt Mina.

"You seem to know my estate rather well," he said finally.

"My friend Gretchen grew up here."

He nodded. "The Winchesters. A nice family."

"Yes, they were. Not that they would have been on Lucy's list of people to invite to your party."

A smile twitched the corner of his mouth. "You don't care for your sister much, do you?"

"I don't care for vanity, cruelty without reason, and frivolity. My sister happens to possess all three of those qualities, making it difficult sometimes." She bit her lip and took a deep breath. "I should not have said that. It was unkind."

"Sometimes the truth is unkind."

She looked up, and to his delight, she smiled. "You aren't at all what I expected."

"And what did you expect?"

She shrugged. "An elderly man. Distinguished and formal. Perhaps a bit stuffy, maybe a tad eccentric."

"Ah, don't judge me so soon, Miss Mina. I have been known to be slightly eccentric at times."

She laughed. "Please call me Mina."

He held his hand out to her. "And you must call me Blue."

She shook his hand, and to his surprise, she didn't mention his chilly pallor. "Is your name really Blue?"

He smiled. "It's not my given name. It's what I've been called since I was a child. First, for my eyes and then because of my hair and beard, which are so black, I am told they hold a blue sheen. What about you? Is Mina your name?"

"Not my given name, no." She tossed him a subtle smile.

"Will you tell me your name?"

"Will you tell me yours?"

"Come to my party this weekend, and I will."

She nodded. "All right. But you must promise not to ask Jonathan my name before then."

He lifted her hand to his lips and sniffed her skin again. The sound of her blood rushing through her veins like a river pounded in his ears. He kissed her knuckles and then smiled at her.

"It's a date."

If his heart still beat, it would have thundered at the intense way she gazed at him. He would have heated from the inside out if his blood had pumped. If he'd been any less of a gentleman, he'd have gathered her in his arms, pressed her into the wall, and kissed her until her legs gave out.

Jonathan pushed through the swinging kitchen, and Mina removed her hand from Blue's. He wanted to strike the young man for interrupting them but managed to hold his anger at bay.

"Mina?" Johnathan questioned.

"I was just looking for you." Mina walked toward him. "Lucy and I need to get home."

Jonathan nodded, but his expression spoke volumes. The anger wafting from him burned Blue's nose like brimstone.

Mina looked over her shoulder. "I shall see you this weekend, then?"

Blue inclined his head, fighting the urge to let Jonathan go for insubordination.

"I cannot wait."

CHAPTER SIX

Mina and Lucy had barely pulled up to the front door when their father stormed out of the house.

"Where have you been?" he demanded.

Jonathan helped Mina from the wagon. "Lucy hurt her ankle when we were on a walk. Count Draugr was kind enough to allow her to rest while she healed."

Her father stared at Lucy as Jonathan helped her from her seat. "Is that so?"

"Yes." Lucy hopped down.

"Which ankle?" he questioned.

Lucy stood for a moment and then limped on her right leg. "This one. I fell on the road. It's quite swollen. But Count Draugr was a wonderful host. And he's having a party this weekend. He invited both Mina and myself."

He looked between them and folded his arms.

"I assure you, sir," said Jonathan. "I did indeed have to pick them up. When I got there, Miss Lucy swooned in my arms."

"Did she indeed?"

Lucy swallowed and looked away.

"Both of you, in the house."

Mina turned to Jonathan and smiled. "Thank you for bringing us home."

Jonathan looked like he wanted to say something, but his gaze traveled to her father. Instead, he bowed and hopped back on the wagon.

Mina and her father watched Lucy try to limp up to the door.

"She would make a terrible actress," her father mused.

Mina smiled. "Especially since she can't even remember which ankle she was limping on earlier."

HER FATHER'S BEDROOM REEKED OF PIPE TOBACCO AND boot polish. Two scents Mina would forever associate with him.

She sat on the edge of his deep-colored wooden, four-poster bed and smoothed his burgundy and gold brocade bedspread as he took his old captain's jacket from its hanger and meticulously folded it.

The heavily shrouded room pressed in around her

as she mulled over the news her father had sprung on them all when she and Lucy had returned home.

"So I will be leaving first thing in the morning and will be gone for no more than thirty days," he announced.

"Thirty days?" said Lucy. "But what are we to do for money?"

He continued packing his bag, placing his boots and shoes on his coat.

"My employer has given me money upfront to ensure you are provided for in my absence." He grabbed his captain's hat and placed it on his bed.

"But Father, you said you would never take a job as a captain. Your dream was owning ships."

He stopped and turned his hardened expression on Lucy. "Sometimes we must sacrifice our dreams to help pay the bills, Lucinda."

Arthur stepped forward. "Then I shall do my part and make sure everything runs smoothly in your absence."

Her father snorted. "You would spend every penny in under a week. No. I trust only one person to look after this house and you lot while I am gone. Andromina."

Her father walked to his dresser and pulled out several pairs of socks as all eyes went to her.

Mina stood. "Me, father?"

He placed the socks in his bag and then put his

hands on her shoulders. "You've kept this house going for over a year now on little to nothing. If it weren't for you, all the lands would have been taken, and everything we own would have been auctioned off to pay our debts. But you kept us afloat, fed, and clothed just as your mother would have. You are the only one I trust."

Mina swallowed hard at the expression on her older siblings' faces. Quincey crushed a cigarette out on his boot and swore under his breath. Arthur's gaze narrowed as much as it could due to the swelling that still marred his eye. On the other hand, Lucy seemed strangely smug, as if she were happy about the news.

A chill slithered down Mina's spine, and she swallowed hard before looking at her father. "I will do my best."

He kissed her head. "I know you will."

"Father, what about the party at Count Draugr's?" asked Lucy. "Are we still allowed to go?"

Mina held her breath. She'd forgotten entirely about Blue in all the excitement. *Please let him say yes.* Just the thought of seeing Blue again made her heart skip. And with her father gone, maybe it was possible she might get to see more of him. Mina's cheeks heated at the thought. It was silly of her to think of such things when she'd only met him once, and it had been... interesting, to say the least.

"You may go—" her father finally said.

Lucy cheered.

"On the condition that your brothers accompany you since I cannot."

Lucy ran to her father and kissed his cheek. "Thank you, Papa."

Mina couldn't remember the last time Lucy kissed their father or called him Papa.

He shooed Lucy off of him and stomped back to his dresser.

"Now out. I must finish packing and getting my things in order before leaving. The coach is coming for me before dawn."

Mina followed her siblings as they filed out of the room. It had been years since her father had gone on a voyage, and she smiled inwardly at the prospect of feeling the weight of his ever-looming presence lifted from her shoulders, even if it was only for a short time.

"Before you go."

The group turned back.

"Upon my return, things will change around here. Arthur, I have secured you a position as a clerk at the National Bank."

Arthur blanched. "A clerk?"

"You will stay with your mother's Aunt Penelope. Work your way up or not. Your life. Your responsibility. But when I return, you must have your bags packed and ready to leave."

"Quincey, an old naval doctor friend, has agreed to take you on at the college where he works. You can take classes there and work as his assistant."

"Medicine?" Quincey questioned.

Their father stopped packing and glared at her brothers. "I've been soft on the two of you for far too long. I see now just how poor a father I've been since your mother's death. First, being away and leaving you with nannies. Then, after retiring, I did not put my foot down. I always wanted to give my children more than I had growing up, but in doing so, I hindered you more than helped. Well, no more. The two of you will either take the positions I've been able to garner you, or you can pack a bag and make your own way in the world. I'm not sending you off in the morning when I leave because there would be no one here to protect the house. Not that I would expect either of you to protect anything but yourselves. Even so, I must do what society deems proper, considering we currently have no house servants. If you don't like those prospects, I suggest you be as charming as possible at the Count's party and try to secure some rich wives while I'm away."

Without another word the siblings continued for the door.

"Andromina?"

Mina stopped.

"Close the door."

Her siblings stared at her again as she shut the

door behind them. She wondered if her father realized the tension he was creating between them.

He sat on his bed and looked at her with a sad smile. "I'm sorry to put this burden on you, but you know that Arthur and Quincey would gamble away the money in a week, and Lucy would spend it on frivolous frocks."

"I understand, Father."

"While I am gone, don't let them bully you. If you have any problems, you remind them that I won't be gone long, and if they do anything to harm or threaten you, I will deal with them accordingly."

"Yes, Father."

He stared at her for a long moment. "Things will change for you upon my return as well. I'm going to hire a maid and a cook. I don't want you having to do that anymore."

"I don't mind," she lied.

"All this time, you've done your duty without complaint and taken on duties that never should have burdened your shoulders. Given me solace where no other could."

"Why the change?" she asked. "Why now?"

He sat silently for a moment. "Because after... the other night and what happened at dinner, I realized I've become my father. A man I swore I would never be. I'm no good sitting at home doing nothing. And since owning ships didn't work out, I need to do the one thing I am good at. Sailing. Even if it means I sail someone else's ships."

Mina nodded. She wondered if his being away and sailing again and her brothers being gone would mean she could finally do things for herself, live a life, and find happiness.

"And one last thing. I want you to go to London and buy yourself a gown for the party this weekend."

Her chest squeezed. "Father, I don't need a new gown."

"You do. You know you do. You are the only one in this house who never asks for anything. You are wearing dresses that your sister has deemed worthless, shoes that are too small for your feet, and a coat that is older than you are. You need a gown and some ribbons for your hair. I want you to go and buy them."

Mina had last bought herself a pair of stockings the year before. The ones she had were so worn that she was better off wearing nothing.

She nodded. "All right."

A new dress. Something just for her... only for Blue to see her in. That was something she could do.

He smiled and then hugged her. It had been a long time since she had seen him smile. "I love you, Andromina. You are the only thing in this world that brings me a moment of happiness."

"I love you too, Papa."

He looked over her, and his eyes misted. "You look so much like your mother."

Mina's brows knit together. "I have always been told I look like you. It's the others who look like Mother."

He nodded. "To others, perhaps that is true. But to me, you are her exact replica."

THAT NIGHT, BLUE REVISITED MINA AS SHE SLEPT. HE flew through her window and melted into the shadows. He'd already set Renfield, as well as the rest of the house staff, to the task of getting ready for the party on Saturday. Including tending to some work on the house's exterior and the inside. He'd gotten a list of people to invite from Jonathan and had begun writing out the invitations. He would rather not have the party, but he couldn't wait to see Mina all dressed up. He imagined what she would look like, hair up off her slender neck, framed in a beautiful gown, her pale skin standing out against all the other women in the room—a dove amongst plain, squawking pigeons.

He moved toward her bed. He only wanted the scent of her hair. Just one sniff, and he would leave her alone until Saturday.

He knelt by her bedside and gently lifted her slender wrist. Her soft skin had his fangs begging for a taste as he focused on the mesmerizing mulberry-colored veins. He lay the pad of his thumb over her pulse and allowed himself to fall into it. The rhythmical *whoosh, whoosh, whoosh* of her blood as it pumped called to him, teased him, tempted him. He lowered his mouth to her wrist, and his fangs dropped into his mouth. Just a taste. A sip to savor and keep him until the weekend.

Suddenly, the door to her room swung open, sending Blue retreated into the murky corner. A tall young man with striking blond hair staggered toward where Mina slept. He stopped at the edge of her bed, bumping into it. Swaying on the spot, he stared at her. The sneer on his face had Blue inching closer, muscles bunching and ready to spring forth. Blue's teeth lengthened further, preparing for the attack.

"It's your fault," the young man slurred. "I am the oldest. I am the one who should be in charge. What makes you so special?"

Her brother, Blue deduced, moved around the side of her. He kicked something on the floor and looked down. Bending, he tried to pick it up and almost fell over. He caught himself on her wobbly nightstand and then stood, clutching a pillow.

"You shouldn't have been so damn good all the time," he said. "We never measured up to you in his eyes. Before you, he at least paid attention to us, but after... mother's death..."

He leaned over Mina, pillow raised.

Blue tensed.

A creak sounded as Mina's door opened a fraction wider.

"What are you doing?" came a strong voice.

The young man turned, dropping the pillow. A burly older man rushed from the door and grabbed Mina's brother by the throat, pinning him to the wall.

"What the hell are you doing, Arthur?" he whispered.

Arthur clawed at the hand on his jugular. "I... I thought I saw her light on."

The larger man lifted Arthur off the floor and slammed him into the wall. "You're drunk." He looked at Mina's sleeping form and then went back to Arthur. "I'm only going to be gone thirty days at most. And if I return and even one hair on her head has been harmed, I'll shoot you myself and bury you in the garden next to your damn dog. Do you understand?"

Arthur nodded vigorously.

"Get the hell out of here before I lose my temper." He tossed Arthur across the room toward the door, but Arthur crashed into her wardrobe and cried out.

Mina stirred, eyes rimmed with sleep. "Father? Arthur?"

Her father turned and smiled. "I just wanted to say goodbye. I'm leaving in the next hour. I'm sorry Arthur woke you. He's drunk as usual."

She sat up. "No. I'm glad he did."

Arthur mumbled an apology and stumbled out.

Her father hugged her tight. "Remember, if you have any problems, let my attorney in London know."

"Of course."

He stared at her for a long moment. "You know where the key to my gun cabinet is?"

Mina laughed, sweet and innocent. "Yes, Father."

"And you remember how to load and shoot as I showed you?"

"Of course, but why would I need to know that?" Her eyebrows crinkled together, making Blue smile.

He touched her cheek. "I just want you safe. No matter who. No matter what. You take care of yourself while I'm gone. And I mean it. Go to London and get yourself a dress for the party."

"But—"

"No arguing."

She nodded, and he kissed her forehead. The tenderness made Blue second-guess his assessment of the man. Was it possible that, like Blue, the man could be both monster and compassionate?

Without another word, her father's face sobered, and he strode out the door.

BLUE WAITED FOR THE BETTER PART OF AN HOUR, watching over Mina, making sure her brother didn't return. He wanted to rip Arthur's throat out. Blue was convinced that Arthur would have tried to smother her if her father hadn't walked in at that moment. Not that he would have succeeded. Blue wouldn't have allowed the lout to harm a single hair on her.

Eventually, the sun's rising tugged on him, forcing him to seek shelter for the day. So, instead of flitting to the next room and ripping her brother apart, he transformed and flew into early morning darkness.

At the forest's edge, his wolves joined him, and they raced back toward his estate together.

He may not have killed her brother, but one thing was clear: Blue needed to get her out of that house—and with her father gone, he needed to do it quick.

CHAPTER SEVEN

The following day, Lucy burst into Mina's room carrying a brightly wrapped package as Mina finished brushing her hair.

"You will never believe it," she squealed.

"What?"

"Look what I got from a secret admirer." Lucy rushed to the bed and plopped onto it. She slid the satin ribbon from the package and opened the lid. Inside lay a gorgeous scarlet-colored silk gown. "Isn't it amazing?"

Mina stared at the expensive material and, for the first time in her life, felt a pang of jealousy that Lucy would once again outshine her. She'd never cared before. To be honest, she'd preferred it that way, but somehow, with Blue, it made Mina green with envy to think that Lucy was setting her sights on the one man who had ever turned Mina's head.

"So the card was addressed to you?" Mina asked.

Lucy's eyebrows smashed together. "What?"

"Didn't it come with a card?"

Lucy licked her lips. "What does that matter?"

"Well, maybe it was a gift for me."

Lucy's mouth fell open, and she stared at Mina like she'd suddenly turned into a teapot. "You? Who would send you a gift like this? Everyone who knows you knows you don't wear things like this."

"Even so. Was there a card?"

Lucy looked away before turning back with a smile on her face. "No. There wasn't."

Anger gurgled inside Mina. It mingled with her jealousy, and suddenly, strength she'd never voiced rose inside her.

"Father told me to go into London and buy a new gown, but he knew I wouldn't, so maybe he got it for me," she blurted.

Lucy's cheeks turned to flames. "And did father say I could also get a new dress?"

Mina didn't wish to hurt her sister, but for the first time, for some unknown reason, she felt that fighting for Blue's attention might be worth an argument.

"He said you have enough dresses."

Lucy rose from the bed and huffed. "So first he puts you in charge of the finances, and then he tells you to buy a gown? What are the rest of us, yester-day's trash?"

The two stared at each other for a tense moment.

Finally, Lucy snatched up the box as if afraid Mina might try and claim it.

"Well, if you are going to get yourself a new dress, then it doesn't matter whose this was supposed to be anyway. You won't need it now that you have all that money in your pocket."

Lucy stormed toward the door and then stopped and turned, her gaze like shards of glass. "Go to London. Get a dress. It won't matter. No one has ever looked at you besides that pitiful doe-eyed twit, Jonathan. And if you do go to London, be sure you don't go at night. I would hate for whoever is killing all those people in the slums down there to mistake you for a lowly wench and drain all the blood out of you too."

With that, Lucy stomped out of the room and slammed the door. Mina's heart drummed wildly. After all she'd done for Lucy and her brothers. Keeping them fed, washing for them, cooking for them, cleaning up after them, tempering her father's wrath, all of it. They didn't care—none of them.

Fine. If they didn't need her, then she most definitely did not need them. Mina's expression hardened as she crossed to her wardrobe, pulled out her cloak, and slipped on her shoes. She refused to back down. Her father had told her that she could buy something new, and that was precisely what she intended to do.

. . .

MINA EXITED THE TRAIN AND TOOK IN THE BUSTLING station. It had been more than a year since she'd traveled to London, and always with her father. Standing alone on the platform, being jostled by the commuters trying to get on the train she'd just vacated, made her stomach clench. She stepped to the middle of the platform as the shrill whistle of the train one track over rang out and smoke billowed into the air. Mina turned around, trying to see where she needed to go, and then turned again as she was moved forward like a fish in a rapidly moving stream. The smell of the ash, the flood of people rushing to their destinations, and the dampness of the air all bombarded her in a way that made her feel like she was being swallowed whole.

A man knocked into her, and Mina almost fell to her knees. Someone grabbed her elbow and set her back on her feet before continuing on. Her heartbeat quickened, and suddenly, her coat was too hot. She needed to get out of there.

Propelled by the crowd, she moved down the ramp and out onto the street to be greeted by the sooty air and skies that looked like God had forgotten his paintbrushes for the day. Moving to the sidewalk, she forced herself to remain calm and get her bearings. The horse-drawn carriages clomp through the wet cobbled streets, the rhythm of their hooves soothing her a touch. She took in the ever-looming brick buildings and the round domed roof of

Paddington Station. After a moment, she remembered where she was and where she needed to be. She took off down the street, heading toward her father's bank.

The further from the station Mina got, the more her shoulders relaxed. She even slowed her pace, mentally noting all the shops she passed that Lucy had dragged her to on previous trips. Seeing the shops lifted her spirits and set her resolve more than ever.

She would go to each one until she found exactly what she desired.

SHE HAD TAKEN OUT ENOUGH MONEY TO PROCURE A dress, a new pair of shoes, and possibly a new coat. And then she had taken out a bit more to pay off Mr. Giles and get her bracelet back. The thought of having the trinket again made her smile.

Mina clutched her purse deep in her coat pocket, being sure not to draw attention to herself. She grabbed a sandwich at a small diner, preparing for a long shopping day.

She headed to the first shop and looked through the window. Inside hung several lovely dresses, but none better than a moderate tea dress, so she moved on, along with the second and third shops. Mina couldn't see anything that she thought might do her justice for the party that weekend making her heart sink a level. She passed a seamstress's shop and paused, but having something made would take far too long.

The afternoon wore on, and the sun began to lower on the horizon as she entered the second-to-last shop. She stopped abruptly as a gorgeous emerald gown called to her from the window. Exceedingly intricate beadwork scattered the bodice, and the small train behind it spoke of its French influences. Never before had she seen something so stunning. Nothing that Lucy had ever worn even compared—not even the red dress that had arrived. The thought pushed the corners of Mina's mouth into a smile.

She opened the shop door and stepped inside. Behind the counter, a man finished wrapping a package for an older woman. Mina nodded to him and then strolled around the shop, touching ribbons and inspecting various items. She waited until the woman left before turning her gaze again to the emerald gown.

"What may I help you with this afternoon, Miss?"

"The dress in the window, what is its price?" She tried to keep her voice as even as possible.

"Beautiful, isn't it? Straight from Paris. Genuine silk with glass beads. It could easily go for fifty dollars or more, but as I've had it for a couple of weeks now, I could let it go for as low as forty-five."

Mina scoffed. "Forty-five? For that price, I could get two just down the street."

"True, but they would never compare in quality."

He was correct, but Mina wasn't about to spend everything she'd taken from the household expenses to pay for a dress, no matter what her father told her.

"Well, then, I thank you for your time." Mina headed for the door. She'd just gotten it open when the man called to her.

"I could do thirty-five."

"Twenty," she countered.

"Twenty-five," he replied.

She could spend another five minutes haggling with him about the price, but she really wanted the dress.

"Twenty-five plus a pair of shoes to match."

The man hesitated only a moment before he smiled. "You won't be disappointed."

She returned his smile. She was sure she wouldn't.

THE RAIN BEGAN SHORTLY AFTER SHE'D FINISHED shopping. Not wanting to ruin the gown and shoes, although they were already in a box, she bought a parasol and headed toward the train station. She reached the station to find a man barring the entrance and turning people away. Mina pressed through the throng to hear what he was saying.

"I'm sorry. I'm sorry. There has been an accident, and all trains out have been suspended until the wreck can be cleared."

"But how long will that take?" a man questioned.

"I don't know. Possibly all night. I suggest everyone turn back to secure lodging."

Mina was surprisingly happy to have an excuse not to go home that night. She wasn't ready to deal with Arthur and Quincey questioning her about the money, asking when she was making food, and trying to con her into giving them a few coins for drinks and cigarettes. She didn't at all want to hear Lucy berating her over and over, wanting to see the gown she'd bought for the party.

Turning from the station, Mina headed back into London. She needed to find a room before everyone else descended on the good hotels. Hustling to the one she'd stayed at many times with her father, the prospect of having an entire room to herself for the night and not having to make the bed or cook and clean for her siblings suddenly appealed to her more than she could put into words.

BLUE PACED HIS ROOM. THE SUN HAD LESS THAN TEN minutes to set, yet he'd been up for over an hour. He couldn't help but worry about Mina and what might befall her now that her father was gone. The idea that she could already be injured had him ready to sink his teeth into any living creature. He'd promised himself that he would not go over before she went to bed, but the anticipation and anxiety had him breaking his own promise. He stared at the clock, watching the seconds tick down. Not that he needed to; the effects of the sun faded with every moment that passed.

He instinctively knew the moment the sun dipped below the horizon, and in an instant, he was out his bedroom window, streaming across the green and through the woods toward her house. He'd make sure she was safe and then return home.

He flitted through the woods, racing alongside his wolves. The crisp night air caressed his face. He breathed in, letting the fresh scent of nature lull away his anxiety. He caught the scent of someone new and halted. He sniffed the air. His wolves growled and turned to the east.

"Stop!" he ordered. The wolves looked to him, their amber eyes radiating through the darkness.

The fragrance was that of a boy. Young, no more than ten or twelve, but slightly familiar. Like the way Harker smelled. A relative, perhaps. His son or a young brother.

"Leave it," he commanded. He couldn't afford for another child to get hurt and bring more unwanted attention his way. He was running out of homes to retreat to.

Blue crept toward Mina's house. Ordering his wolves to return to their den for the night.

Floating toward her balcony, he stopped beside it and grabbed onto the wall. He hung silently, listening to voices deep in conversation.

"I told you she was gone, Quincey," said Lucy. "Did you think I would make that up?"

"What happened? Where did she go?"

"I don't know, but if I had to guess, I would say to London."

"Why would she go there?"

"Father told her to buy a dress for the party this weekend. He told her she could use some of the money he left for all of us on herself."

"What is this party you keep going on about," asked Arthur. Blue recognized the man from the night before.

"Count Draugr is having a party and invited us."

"Father said we were to take them," said Quincey. "That is if Mina comes back. It's not like her to stay away. Are you sure you didn't say or do something, Lucy?"

"Why would you think I did something?"

"Because you can't help but be jealous of her."

Lucy huffed. "Jealous? Of Mina? Don't be simple. What do I have to be jealous of her for?"

"Stop!" said Arthur. If Mina doesn't come back, when Father returns, our hides will pay."

"The way he loves that girl is nothing to be trifled with."

"It's only because she looks like-"

"Even so," said Quincey. "She better get back right quick. Soon, Lady Crawford's husband will find out she's pregnant."

"Tell Lady Crawford to pay for her own abortion. Lord Crawford finding out you fathered a bastard by his wife is nothing compared to what I will have to deal with if I can't get my hands on some of that money," replied Arthur.

"Lady Crawford can't touch a pence without accounting for it to her husband. So if I don't figure something out soon, I'm as good as dead."

"Didn't Father say he'd arranged a job for you as a doctor? Maybe you could learn to do the abortion yourself." Lucy chuckled.

"You're such a bitch, Lucy."

"It's your own fault for being so stupid as to sleep with a woman whose husband can't get her pregnant," Arthur scoffed. "Anyway, at least you'd go quick in a duel. I owe money on the last four card games I've played. If I don't give back the money, you'll have to pay a heap ton for the mortician to make me recognizable for my funeral."

"You're both idiots who have caused your own problems. What about me? I'm innocent in all of this," said Lucy.

Quincey snorted. "I highly doubt that."

"You both better hope that serial killer in London doesn't get to her first and bleed her dry," Lucy snapped.

Blue lifted into the sky. Mina was at least safe from her siblings for the moment, and she had nothing to fear from him.

But that didn't mean she was safe in London.

BLUE RACED AGAINST THE WIND AS HE FLEW IN THE clouded sky. He sniffed the city air, searching for her scent as he landed on the Tower of London. A shiver raced over his skin. He'd done his best to avoid densely populated areas for over a hundred years. Going to the slums of London meant he was less likely to be seen, and the people were more than likely not to be missed. But to find Mina, he'd have to go somewhere completely different. He'd have to head to the districts where, when a woman went missing, the police got involved. The districts where people noticed what you wore and who you were. But for her, he would be willing to tempt fate and then some.

He scanned as far as he could and inhaled deeply. A million different scents floated through his nostrils within seconds. He caught them all, dismissing them in turn until he caught the scent of peonies and mint. His eyes focused on a hotel on the upper side of the city. She was there.

Blue flew to the hotel and dropped down into the alleyway next to it, transforming back into human form. He straightened his jacket and vest before striding from the alley and heading to the hotel entrance. He stopped at the bottom step and combed his fingers through his hair. He had no idea what to say when he saw her, but he didn't care. All he wanted was to be close to her.

Blue strode up the steps and headed inside. The bright marble and highly polished oak made him squint as he continued through the lobby, allowing his nose to lead him. He halted at the entrance of the restaurant and scanned the room. At a small table, she ate alone. For several moments, he savored her ubiquitous movements. The way she cut small portions of her meat and chewed them deliberately. The way she smiled and thanked the waiter. The way her delicate fingers grasped her wine glass as she sipped from it. He wished to feel those same graceful fingers running over his skin, touching his face, gripping his back as he made love to her.

A young man walked to her table and spoke to her, breaking the spell.

"I'm sorry," said Mina. "I'm not really up for company."

The man said something else, pulled out the chair, and sat.

The look on Mina's face told Blue that she was not impressed. Blue strolled into the restaurant, moving closer to them.

Mina sat her fork down on her plate and tucked her hands in her lap. "I'm sorry, sir. I am afraid I really must ask you to leave. Please don't make me get the waiter."

"Don't be like that. I simply want to offer you

some company. You look so lonely. How is it that a beautiful girl like yourself doesn't have an escort?"

Blue made for the table and stood at her side. "She does have an escort."

Mina looked up at him, her eyes wide.

Blue bent down and kissed her cheek, taking a moment to catch the quickening of her heartbeat. "Sorry to have been so long in my meeting, darling. Will you ever forgive me?"

A coy smile crinkled the corners of Mina's eyes. "I will not. This is the third time this week you have kept me waiting. I was about to take this young man up on his offer. Obviously, he values my company enough to allow me not to dine alone. Isn't that right?"

Mina turned to the young man who looked between them.

"I... well..."

"Oh, please," Blue teased, playing along. "I promise if you will forgive me this one last time, I will never leave you alone again."

Mina's eyes sparkled with mischief as she turned to the young man. "You would never leave me waiting, would you?"

"I... I... would try not to." He fiddled with his jacket, and his muscles bunched as if to make a hasty retreat.

"And if you did, you would certainly buy me a tremendous gift, wouldn't you? Flowers, chocolates, a new frock even."

"That... sounds reasonable," the young man offered.

"Well, I can't afford all that, I'm afraid. It's obvious you could do much better. This young man surely could give you everything you desire with his expensive coat and cravat tied so meticulously. I have no choice but to do the gentlemanly thing and leave you to him." Blue bowed to her and then looked at the young man. "Goodbye, my love. I wish you the best of luck. And, before you leave, would you be so good as to pay her tab?"

"Her tab?"

"Yes, between the room and food, I believe her bill is close to one hundred pounds here at the hotel. And then the dress shop is owed another fifty pounds. And the jeweler—"

"You know, I just remembered I need to be somewhere." The young man stood and dashed for the door.

Mina and Blue watched him go, and then Blue laughed.

"I suppose that's one way to get rid of a man."

"Thank you for playing along."

"Do you think *I* have earned a seat at your table?"

She nodded. "If you'd like."

Blue took the empty seat, and the waiter headed over. "Can I get you something, sir?"

"Just some red wine, please."

The waiter nodded.

Mina stared at him for a moment. "So what brings you to London?"

"Business. I happened to be staying in the hotel, and I saw you sitting here and decided to say hello. Seems a good thing I did. Does that happen frequently?"

"What?"

"Young men forcing their company on you?"

She looked down at her plate. "Not often."

"I have a hard time believing that."

"It's Lucy who is usually inundated with attention."

He studied her for a moment. "You don't seem to mind that."

Mina shrugged. "I don't have time for flirting, primping, and doing everything needed to obtain a husband."

"Don't have time, or don't have the patience?"

The corner of her mouth curved upward. "Why is it women feel they need to fancy up and strut around like peacocks to catch a man? Why can't men care more about what's inside? What she thinks, desires, dreams."

Blue leaned across the table, setting his hand next to hers. "What do you dream, Mina?"

Her cheeks tinged with pink. "Surely you aren't interested in that?"

"Why not?"

"Because..." She looked at her plate and twirled her fork.

He didn't want to pressure her, but he truly wanted to know every single thing about her.

"Do you want to know what I dream of?"

Her gaze lifted. The thumping of her rapid heartbeat thrummed in his ears.

"Yes," she whispered.

"I dream of distant lands. Of living in hotels like this. Of traveling with one woman by my side for eternity. Just the two of us, owning the world together."

The way she stared at him, her gaze full of longing and need, made him ache to turn her and make her his.

"Your wine, sir?" The waiter arrived.

Blue sat back as the waiter set the glass down.

Mina twirled a strand of hair around her finger.

"So," he finally asked. "What do you dream?"

She continued to look at him for another minute before finally saying, "I dream of adventure."

Blue smiled, and Mina smiled as well. More than ever, his heart told him that she was the one.

CHAPTER EIGHT

Mina could scarcely believe Blue had swooped in like a guardian angel to save her from being pressured by the young man. And then he'd wanted to stay and spend time with her. It all seemed surreal. London was a bustling city. What were the odds that he'd run into her? Even slimmer odds that they'd be staying in the same hotel. Probably slimmer still, considering that until that morning, she hadn't even known she would be headed to London, and not until that evening that she'd known she would be staying the night. For a split second, she wondered if fate brought them together. Then, she reminded herself that she didn't believe in fate.

They spoke about the world, life, and books for over an hour. She found it amazingly refreshing to talk with a man about such things and not be judged for having thoughts, opinions, and dreams more than having children and organizing house staff.

He sat through her entire meal, watching her eat while sipping his glass of wine. His pitch-black hair and pale skin brightened his blue eyes in the dim candlelight.

"Well," Mina finally said. "I believe I have prattled on long enough. I should let you go—"

"Would you mind accompanying me on a walk? I'd like to show you something."

Mina's heartbeat pattered like a sparrow's. "I don't know. There have been several murders here of late. It could be dangerous."

He leaned forward and held his hand out to her. "I assure you, no harm will come to you while I am here."

Everything inside her wanted to take it. To feel his grip on her skin. To have his fingers entwined with hers.

She nodded but didn't take his hand. "All right."

Blue smiled and snapped his fingers. The waiter arrived immediately, and Blue handed him several bills. When Mina protested, he shook his head.

"Where I come from, we would never allow a beautiful woman to pay for her meal when she had graced us with the pleasure of stimulating conversation."

Mina stared at him for a moment. "Are you mocking me, sir?"

Blue's eyebrows drew together. "Mocking you how?"

He appeared genuine in his compliment about the conversation.

"Never mind."

He rounded the table and helped her from her chair. He leaned in close, and she caught the manly fragrance of his aftershave.

"I would never mock you, Mina. I hope you know at least that much about me. I am genuine in my attention."

Mina swallowed hard at the nearness of his body. He stepped away and offered her his arm instead.

Together, they walked out of the hotel and down the dim street. The gas lamps were just beginning to be lit along the way. The rain had stopped, and everything smelled of damp stone and earth.

"I love that smell," she said. "It's like new life. God cleansing away the sins of the day."

"You believe in God?"

"I've never really given it much thought before. My nanny was a believer, and she took us to church. I listened and absorbed the priest's words. I never really questioned it, I suppose."

He was quiet for a moment.

"Does that bother you?" she asked.

"I find it interesting. You seem to question everything else."

It was true, but for that, she felt there was no need to question. It just was.

They rounded the corner and stopped in front of an extravagant building with a giant flashing marquee. The light bulbs shone through the settling fog, beckoning them forward.

Cooper and Edelstein's House of Oddities twinkled brightly above her.

"They have a moving picture show inside," said Blue.

"I've never seen one before."

He smiled, revealing bright white teeth. "Wonderful, then I will be the one to help you experience it."

He pulled her forward and paid for two tickets at the booth before entering. Inside, the bright lights of electricity made her blink. Despite all of the advancements in London, she still preferred candlelight. The smell of chemicals, bodies, and animals hit her nose in an odd combination.

A crowd of people milled about, gawking and pointing at different exhibits. People clapped and cheered to her left, but Mina couldn't see what they watched. Some gasped, and a woman screamed as fire burst into the air. Mina grabbed onto Blue, and he patted her hand.

They continued into the building, and Mina didn't know where to go first; there were so many new and unusual things. Glass cases, cages, displays, and more encompassed the sizable warehouse-like floor. Statues of famous people. Stuffed animals from far-off places. Gadgets and gizmos of all kinds whirled and clanged and sputtered. Mina stopped momentarily at a stage with a significant banner reading, *Can we Raise the Dead?* She watched in wrapt fascination as a man standing attached electrodes to a frog, and the dead animal twitched, flipped to its feet, and croaked.

Mina gasped as the crowd cheered. "Did you see that?"

Blue steered her to the left and pointed at an enormous woman perched on a stool with a beard dripping down her chin. Next to her, the tallest man Mina had ever seen lifted a tiny man, no bigger than a toddler, in the palm of his hand. A pair of brothers joined at the chest, waved to the crowd, and smiled before breaking into a dance. Finally, a woman covered in tattoos draped a thick, shiny snake over her shoulders as she danced.

Each person intrigued her more than the last.

"What do you think?" Blue asked.

"They are amazing," Mina responded. "I just wonder why they choose to be here. Do they enjoy the attention, or is the pay such that they can't refuse?"

She regarded the performers as more and more customers pointed and gawked. Some laughed or jeered, making Mina want to shout at them.

"You're not like other people," said Blue.

She turned to look at him. "Yes, I am."

He chuckled. "It's a compliment. You see those

other people? See the way they look at the performers. They don't see people. They see things. Pets. Toys.
Oddities. You see people. Human beings deserving of
love and respect."

"Because that's what they are."

He pointed at a man who threw an apple at the
fat lady and laughed.

"Not to everyone."

Blue pulled her onward.

Next, they came upon an exhibit of exotic
animals. Birds, monkeys, a bear and tiger, and, finally,
a giant white wolf snarled at people as they passed.
Blue stopped in front of the animal's cage, and it
looked at him and snapped its jaws.

Blue left her side without a word and walked
closer to the cage. The animal bared its teeth, but
then suddenly, its posture eased, and it sat.

"How strange." She moved to Blue's side.

The animal jumped back to its feet and growled at
her. Blue stepped between them, and the animal
calmed as if answering a command.

"How did you do that?"

Blue turned to her and took her arm. "As with all
animals, you just need to make sure they know who
the boss is."

A voice came over a loudspeaker. "The magical
moving picture will start in five minutes in the rear
theater."

He smiled at her and patted her hand. "Come."

They walked past several exhibits, but when they got to the medical section, fascination called Mina toward the encasements.

In a bell jar filled with greenish fluid floated a two-headed monkey. And on display next to it was the skeleton of a baby with three arms. They walked on with one thing after another, drawing Mina's eye. She spotted an entire cabinet of skulls and pulled Blue toward it.

"I've never seen a real human skull before," she said.

"They don't frighten you?"

She looked at him quizzically. "Why would they?" She moved down the case, noticing the subtle differences between the skulls. Some were tiny, like babies or small children. Others enormous and misshapen. One had a huge forehead and tiny facial features. Several had heavy protruding jaws. She stopped as she got to the end.

"Is that real? Surely, no human could have teeth that long." The skull had two long, sharp fangs jutting from its top jaw.

"Maybe it's not a human," Blue suggested.

Mina laughed, but his expression remained serious. "You're joking, of course."

"There are millions of animals in this world. Billions of human beings. Seven continents, some not completely explored. What's to say that there aren't other species of humans out there? Or something like humans, but not completely human."

"But where would they come from? Evolution? Surely God would not have created something like that."

"There you are again with God. You shouldn't believe everything you are told."

She laughed. "Does that include what you tell me?"

His mischievous smile made his eyes crinkle. "Most definitely."

The intensity of his gaze made her wonder what he meant.

"Well then, I should be extra careful in your company lest I let you beguile me."

A strange feeling came over her. As if everyone in the world faded away and there was no one but the two of them. Blue's face came into sharp focus as their surroundings vanished into a mist of clouds. His arm slipped around her waist. The coolness of his touch seeped through her clothing, but she didn't mind the sensation. He pressed her body into his in an intimate embrace. No words were exchanged, but desire floated off him as if he'd spoken it out loud. Mina's pulse raced, and even as her head told her that she shouldn't let him touch her so intimately, her body fully approved. His fingers brushed her cheek, and she closed her eyes.

His body wrapped around hers, and every particle

of her focused on Blue. The way his hand splayed on the small of her back. The firmness of his arm as it cradled her. The smoothness of his knuckles as he stroked her cheek. The thickness of his glossy mustache.

The prickle of his cool breath washed over her throat. She stiffened in anticipation, but of what, she had no idea. A kiss? His breath? Something else?

An impassioned thrill raced over her skin as if something was coming for her. Something right around the bend. A new life. A new dream. A new adventure. Frenzied and ominous like a thunderstorm. Yet illuminating as a lightning strike. She waited for him to do something, anything. She leaned into him, her only desire to become his.

Without warning, everything around her crashed back, and she stood in the middle of the exhibit. Blue no longer held her in his arms but stood a foot from her, looking at the skulls. Like disembarking a merry-go-round too quickly, Mina fought to catch her bearings as the room around her spun. Noises blared, lights blinded, and smells overwhelmed her.

She glanced around, completely off-kilter. As she teetered sideways, Blue grabbed her arm.

"Are you all right?" His eyes held concern.

"Uhm... I'm not sure." She wiped her brow, trying to understand what had happened.

The sensation was eerily similar to what had happened to her the first day she'd spotted him in the carriage. The feeling of a fog in her head and then slamming back into the world. Was something wrong with her? Was she ill?

"I... I think maybe I should get going." She stumbled away from him.

"But I haven't shown you the moving picture show."

"Thank you, but... I need to leave."

"Mina, let me walk you."

She waved him off, uncertain of what was happening. All she knew was that she didn't want to embarrass herself in front of him.

"I...I can go by myself. Thank you for the lovely evening." She turned and dove into the crowd.

"Mina!"

She heard her name but continued moving anyway. A shiver traced her spine, and she suddenly needed to return to her room as swiftly as possible.

MINA DISAPPEARED, AND BLUE CURSED HIMSELF FOR having gone too far with her too quickly. He shouldn't have used his influence on her like that. Instead of drawing her closer, he'd scared her. He wanted to go after her, to explain and apologize, but he wasn't even sure she knew what had happened. Telling her now would push her away, and he couldn't risk that.

"Five minutes until closing," announced a voice

overhead. "Please begin making your way to the exits, and thank you for visiting."

Five minutes? How long had they been standing there? Blue continued tracking Mina as she made her way through the front door and out to the street. He wanted to follow her and make sure that she was safe. But he had something he needed to take care of first.

People filed out of the museum, and Blue followed behind until he reached the live exhibit. Walking to the wolf's cage, he blended into the shadow as the lights overhead began to extinguish. He headed to the back of the cage, and the wolf tracked him to the door. Blue looked at the padlock and gripped it in his fist. Squeezing, he twisted the lock off and undid the latch. The door swung outward, and he called to the wolf. It looked at him for a moment and then jumped to the floor. Blue pet the wolf's head.

"Come, my friend. You do not belong in a cage."

Keeping to the dimly lit parts of the exhibits, Blue strode to the exit with the wolf in his wake. They hit the door and slipped out behind a buxom woman and her brood of scraggly children.

On the somber streets, the rain had begun to fall once more, washing away the stench of the city, but he caught Mina's scent. She'd headed toward the hotel.

Mina awoke later than she ever had. She'd slept so soundly that not even the knock of the morning maids had awakened her. Instead, she slept almost until noon and ordered breakfast in her room. Mina did not need frivolity, but the silence and the knowledge that she didn't have to tend to her siblings refreshed her more than she could have imagined.

While munching on her toast, she tried to recall how she'd gotten back to the hotel the night before. It had all been a blur since shortly after seeing the skulls in the oddity museum. She didn't remember saying goodnight to Blue or him walking her to the hotel or... anything. The idea frightened her. She hoped she hadn't been rude to him in some way, or worse that she'd had too much wine at dinner and made a fool of herself.

She replayed the night a million times and finally gave up trying to remember.

Late that afternoon, she stood at the side of the bed, looking at her packages and willing herself to pick them up, get on the train, and go home—but she couldn't. She wanted to stay in London and have a few more moments of peace. She knew too well what going home would bring: yelling, demanding, coercion, and, worse, begrudging stares and seething resentment because her father had left her in charge.

She wasn't having it. Not this time. She refused to

apologize for finally doing something for herself. If she was going to be yelled and sniped at, she might as well make it worth it. She would stay in London until the party. She wondered if she should send a letter or a telegram. In the end, she decided they probably wouldn't care anyway.

MINA SPENT THE NEXT THREE DAYS BEING AS conservative with her budget as possible but simultaneously enjoying herself. She spent her mornings in bed, her afternoons at museums and the library, or walking the streets and just taking everything in. She ate dinner alone in the evenings, though Blue was never far from her thoughts. She found herself hoping that he would show up at any moment and whisk her off again.

When he hadn't returned by the third day, she'd gone to see the moving picture by herself. She enjoyed it but knew it would have been made much more marvelous by sharing the experience with him. Somehow, though, she'd felt like he'd been there with her, just out of view, so she'd spent at least half her time looking for him and expecting him to step out of the dark velvet curtains and sit right next to her. It was silly. He was a Count and had better things to do than to escort her around London, showing her sights. But she'd not felt more connected or intellectually stimulated by anyone in her life than she had been by him for those few hours. That knowledge made his absence all the more painful.

THE HOUR DREW CLOSER FOR THE PARTY, AND MINA dressed at the hotel. In her last few moments alone, she suddenly became nervous about returning to her home and, more specifically, Blue's party. She felt like her time with him had been no more than a dream and possibly hadn't even happened. But that was nonsense. She hadn't hallucinated him. However, what if something had happened, and she'd inadvertently pushed him away? She reined in her thoughts to keep them from spinning out of control, but as she made her way to the train station in the beautiful gown she'd bought, she became painfully aware of how people stared at her. It made her want to run and hide.

Mina bought her ticket home and stared at the train. Something whispered to her that if she boarded it and went to the party, her life would change forever. Chills blanketed her skin at the prospect.

CHAPTER NINE

Blue stood in his lavish ballroom, watching the people laugh, dance, and steal glances in his direction. Waiters passed around trays of champagne, and an entire table full of food stood on the side of the room where people grazed like chattering sheep. It pleased him how much they'd accomplished on the house in such little time.

The inside downstairs had been repainted, as had the shutters. The carpets had been beaten and cleaned. The woodwork scrubbed and oiled, making everything smell of oranges. Even the rosebushes had been trimmed back along the entrance, and the fallen chimney had been carted away. Though it wasn't perfect, the house looked decades younger than it had upon his arrival.

Blue stood apart from the masses, watching people he didn't know or care about eat his food. Look at his artwork. And drink his champagne. A knot wound tight in his gut at the prospect of having so many people in his house at once, but it was a means to an end. If he invited them in, they were less likely to talk about him negatively behind his back. That alone was worth its price in anxiety. Another most apparent reason was to have a valid reason to see Mina and spend time with her.

However, the party had started an hour before, and she had yet to arrive. He knew she was safe because he'd watched her every evening from the darkened hideaways of London.

He'd followed her as she'd strolled the streets looking in shop windows but never buying anything. And he'd smiled from the corner as she'd purchased a small bouquet of violets from an old beggar woman, giving her twice as much money as she'd asked for. He'd been behind her as she watched the moving picture show and had fought the urge to show himself and sit next to her. To taste her neck and smell her skin. She'd looked over her shoulder so many times that, at one point, he could almost swear she knew he hid there.

Finally, every night, though, the cravings had become too much for him. And when he feared he might lose control and bite her, he'd rushed away.

The desire building inside him had become almost consuming as the nights had carried on. She made him feel and think of things he hadn't experienced in over five hundred years. She made him yearn to be gentle. Made him fight to be witty. Challenged his ideas and made him ponder important global matters. Forced him to push past his carnal lusts and work to form a connection with her. He had no idea why she succeeded, as so many had tried and failed before— he only knew that she'd awakened something inside him. A part of his humanity he'd sworn he'd lost. And for that, he had to have her.

Blue's gaze moved to a new group of people as they entered. Lucy stood in the doorway, flanked by two young men. Arthur, he recognized from Mina's bedroom, though at the time, he hadn't caught the black eye in its late stages of healing. The younger man, he assumed, was their other brother, Quincey.

Blue gripped his glass tightly and fought not to break it as Lucy removed her cloak. She wore an expensive, blood-red dress cut low in the front and bustled with yards and yards of silk fabric in the rear. A dress that cost more than she could afford—a dress that Blue had hand-picked himself and sent to Mina. Yet, Mina was not in it. His anger spiked, and he tried to set the wine glass on the mantle next to him, but it cracked. The glass broke into pieces and dripped rich burgundy liquid through his fingertips. A sliver of glass sliced his finger. Fat droplets of blood welled upon his skin. He flung the shards into the fire and pulled out his handkerchief.

He looked up again and sucked the blood from his

finger. His fangs lengthened a fraction, but he wrapped the handkerchief around his finger and forced them to retract. Lucy headed straight for him, a broad smile on her rouged lips. Blue gritted his teeth as she approached and gave a deep curtsy, showing off her peachy cleavage.

"Count."

Blue's gaze darted to the two brothers, who resembled Lucy closely. They had light hair, peachy skin, and pale eyes—nothing like his beautiful Mina.

Blue inclined his head. "Miss Lucy."

Lucy turned to her brothers. "May I introduce my elder brother, Arthur, and my younger brother, Quincey?"

Blue nodded to them in turn. "Gentlemen. Welcome."

"Thank you," said Arthur. "You have a beautiful estate. It's been many years since I've been over. We used to fox hunt with the Lord who resided here previously. Great fox hunting on your lands."

Blue shrugged. "I wouldn't know. I don't hunt foxes."

"We should go sometime," offered Quincey. "I'm sure you would love it."

Blue gave a pleasant smile. "I prefer to hunt a more... elusive prey." He looked at Lucy in the gown meant for Mina and couldn't keep the words in his mouth. "That frock, Miss Lucy, wherever did you get it?"

"Isn't it glorious?" She beamed. "A secret admirer sent it to me."

"I would have thought someone admiring you would have known you'd look much better in a lighter color. A deep color like that I would have thought favored your sister better."

Lucy's cheeks flushed, and Blue had to keep himself from smiling at his words' effect. Renfield arrived with a single glass of red wine. Blue took it and placed the stained handkerchief on his tray. The wound on his finger was already healing.

"Problem, sir?" Renfield asked.

"My glass broke. Nothing to worry about, but if you could get Iona to clean up the mess, I would be most appreciative."

Renfield bowed and headed toward the door.

"Where is your sister Mina?" Blue sipped his wine. "I was under the impression she would be attending as well."

He looked over the siblings as they exchanged glances.

"To be honest, we aren't sure where she is," said Lucy.

"Is she missing?"

"She left a few days ago after a small argument, and we haven't heard from her," replied Arthur.

Blue looked between them again. Did they care nothing for their younger sister? "Have you informed the constable?"

"We didn't want to bother them." Quincey coughed.

"I'm quite sure she has just gone to London to get away for a few days," Lucy interjected. "She does that from time to time."

Blue saw the lie for what it was. Mina had told him she hadn't been to London in over a year. He could hardly believe they would be so callous as not to question their younger sister's whereabouts.

"London has become quite dangerous of late. I would think you'd be more concerned. Attempted rapes, murders, and robberies. A girl of her delicacy would surely be a target. Have you not gone there to see if you can find her?"

Arthur and Quincey looked away, and Lucy's cheeks flushed so violently she appeared as if she might burst.

A young man approached the group and shook hands with Arthur and Quincey.

"I don't mean to interrupt," he said. "But I wondered if Miss Lucy would care to dance."

Blue smiled at the young man. "By all means."

Conflicted Lucy looked to him, but Blue simply nodded her direction and sipped his wine. Eventually, she took the young man's hand and sauntered on the dance floor.

Blue turned his gaze on the two brothers, who squirmed under his scrutiny. He fought the urge to leave the party and fly to find Mina at that very moment. She wouldn't possibly stand him up, would she? He gulped down his wine and looked at the clock. Only time would tell if he'd successfully reeled her in or scared her away for good.

MINA STEPPED OFF THE TRAIN AND ONTO THE platform. The smell of London left her head with a breath of the refreshing country air. A part of her wanted to get back on the train, empty the bank account her father had left them, and use the money to disappear. But that would be wrong. No matter how spoiled her siblings were, they didn't deserve to be left destitute. And the heartbreak it would cause her father was something she could never live with. Besides... more than anything, she had to find out what had happened with Blue. Good or bad, she needed to know. Raising her chin, she walked down the platform to the road beyond.

She reached the steps, and Charlie hopped off a coach and hurried toward her.

"Mina Beana."

"Charley Barley, what are you doing down here?"

"I came with Jonathan to pick you up." Charlie grinned large as a crescent moon and gave her a deep bow before moving to the carriage and opening the door.

"Wow, you came." Jonathan smiled as he hopped from the coachman's seat.

"Why are you here?"

Jonathan took the box with her other clothes inside and placed it in the coach.

"Count Draugr said you would be arriving on the train tonight, and I was to wait here until you showed up. I've been here almost three hours. I was beginning to lose hope. Good thing I had Charlie and his stories to keep me company. Are you all right? What were you doing in London alone?"

Usually, she would have told Jonathan everything about her father leaving, the money, her fight with Lucy, all of it. But something stopped her. In the past days, she'd learned she could stand on her own two feet. No longer overshadowed by Lucy. And out from under her father's thumb, she'd begun to rediscover what it felt like to be herself. For the first time in a long time, she thought about her future and what she wanted. And as much as she hated to destroy his hopes, Jonathan was not that future. She needed to distance herself from him and his friendship if she had any hope of letting him down gently.q

"Father took a job as a captain of a ship. I needed to see his banker to get money for supplies while he's gone."

How had Blue known she hadn't gone home and would need a ride from the train station that night? The thought warmed her insides to see he'd sent her a coach. It meant that she hadn't done something to upset him the night they'd gone to the museum.

"Well, I'm glad you're safe, what with there being another two murders there this week. That makes ten in total over the last two weeks."

"I had no idea there were so many," she replied, walking to the coach.

"Didn't you read the newspaper?"

Mina shook her head. "I've never taken to reading it. I prefer books to the paper."

Jonathan looked her up and down. "You look beautiful. I don't remember seeing that dress before. It couldn't be one of Lucy's. She'd never give something like that up."

Mina swallowed hard, remembering the crimson gown Lucy had claimed for herself. "No. It's new."

Charlie stepped up and offered his hand. Mina took it and stepped into the plush black coach.

"Thank you, kind sir."

Charlie giggled and Jonathan nodded for Charlie to get in the front seat.

The curtains inside the coach completely blocked out the light. She wondered if Blue traveled often and liked to sleep in the coach.

Jonathan stood at the door for a moment.

"What's wrong?"

He opened and closed his mouth, looked over his shoulder, and then opened it again. "I want you to be careful tonight."

"Careful? Of who, Lucy?"

Jonathan shook his head. "I don't think the Count is who we imagined him to be."

Mina's gut twisted. "Did something happen?"

"It's nothing that's happened. It's just who he is. He's secretive and spends his time completely alone. Keeps strange hours and never seems to leave the house. Though honestly, he could be gone most of the time, and I'd never know because he only lets Renfield attend him, and he is usually locked in his study or his room like he's hiding from the world. He had us scrubbing and painting all week. Yet when one of the workmen tried to go into his study, he flew into a violent rage and told us all that we were forbidden from entering there. It was quite startling."

Jonathan's words surprised Mina. Did they know the same person? Blue hadn't been that way at all with her. He'd been open and friendly, jovial even.

"I know it sounds like I'm being foolish, but I tell you, there is something strange about him, and it scares me."

"Then why don't you leave?"

"I'd have to leave for London or somewhere further off to find a job half as good with not nearly as substantial a wage. Besides, who would help Mom look after Charlie."

The words he didn't say hung in the air. He didn't go because of her because of the hope that she would someday consent to marry him. The problem was, now more than ever, she knew that could never happen. Even if her feelings for Blue went no further than just friendship, she would never be able to marry Jonathan. He would always be more of a brother than a lover. The way being with Blue had awakened her made her realize what she wanted out of life. And he let her know it was possible to find a man willing to accept her just as she was. If nothing else, he deserved to be thanked for that.

She smiled at Jonathan. "Thank you for your concern, but I can care for myself."

Jonathan closed the door and headed to the front of the coach. He slapped the reins against the midnight-colored stallions, and they lurched forward.

Mina's heart beat like a hummingbird's knowing that soon she would be back in Blue's house, but this time surrounded by other society people—and more importantly, her siblings.

JONATHAN PULLED TO THE FRONT DOOR AND STOPPED the coach. Mina fidgeted with her beads while waiting for him to open the door. She'd loved how she looked when she put on the gown, but now, about to reveal herself to everyone she knew, her nerves suddenly got the better of her.

The door opened, and Jonathan held his hand out. This was the moment. If she didn't want to face everyone, she needed to tell him to drive her home.

She opened her mouth to say the words but stopped. If she turned back now, though, she wasn't sure she'd ever have the nerve to try again. She thought of Blue. He'd invited her. It would be rude of her to not at least make an appearance and thank him for his invitation.

Mina swallowed hard and took Jonathan's hand. He helped her out, and his rough hand lingered for a moment.

"Try to remember who you are, Mina," he said.

"What do you mean?"

"I just..." He looked toward the front of the house and then back at her. "I want you to remember how unique and special you are. You don't have to be like them. You are wonderful just the way you are."

Mina leaned in and kissed his cheek. "Thank you for that. See, this is why you are my best friend. You know just what I need to hear."

A moment passed between them, and Jonathan leaned closer as if to kiss her. Mina tumbled backward into the carriage, making the horses whinny.

"I... I should get going," she said. "You can leave my things in the coach. I'll get them on my way out."

Jonathan's eyes drooped with sadness. "Of course."

She let go of his hand and walked up the steps to the open front door, shoulders back, head held high. If she were to embarrass herself completely, she would do it magnificently.

"Have fun!" Charlie called.

Mina looked over her shoulder at him and waved. Then she strode through the front door, and a maid took her cloak. She straightened her sleeves and fought the urge to pinch her cheeks. She was who she was, and people would either accept her or not. There wasn't much she could do about it now.

Mina's fingers fidgeted as she floated toward the melodious dance music. She peeked around the open doors to see the room full of people. She spotted Lucy dancing with Lord Manchester's son, Alfred. Good. At least she wouldn't have to deal with Lucy right away. She scanned the room as she walked through the door, trying to spot Blue. She pretended not to notice the whispers and stares of the men and women as they spotted her, but like the buzz of a beehive, word seemed to spread around the room about her, and soon everyone who wasn't dancing turned her direction... and then she spotted him.

Standing by the fireplace in a long fitted jacket that matched his hair, a glass of wine between his fingers. He stood with other men who chattered at him, pandering for his praise. Praise Mina knew he would never give because the men were not worthy. Blue went to sip his wine and stopped mid-drink. His gaze moved to hers like magnets pulling on each other, forcing them together.

Her ribcage squeezed tighter than the corset that already bound her, and again, a fog overcame her. As if sucked forward in a vortex, everything else fell away, and he stood directly in front of her. Every nerve in her body tingled at the scent of his cologne. Like a giddy idiot, she remained speechless at his brilliant smile.

She held perfectly still as he circled her, his soft yet icy hand tracing across her collarbone, shoulder, and throat. Goosebumps pebbled her skin, making her chill and flush at the same time. His touch lingered on her skin, gentle but firm.

He stopped behind her, and his arm encompassed her waist. She dared not even breathe at the feel of him. His hard body pressed into her back, making her weak with wanting him. His fingertips tilted her face to look back at his. All fear of what may or may not have happened that night in the museum fell away, and at the moment, she wanted nothing more than to feel his lips on hers.

His gaze burned into her with a heat intense enough to force her to look away. She realized how much she'd missed him in the few days of his absence. How her body ached to feel his presence. How her ears longed to hear the deep timber of his voice. How her eyes craved the sight of his face.

How was it even possible that she could miss a person she barely knew so incredibly much when he was not around?

A firm grip on her arm shook her from her fog, and the present slammed back on her. The music invaded her ears, and the prying eyes of everyone in attendance at the party pierced her where she stood in the entrance to the ballroom.

Mina regarded Arthur, whose grip tightened on her arm.

"What are you doing? You look like a fool," he hissed.

She didn't recognize him for a moment, and then the icy splash of reality slapped her once more.

"Let go of me," she whispered, trying to jerk away. "You have no right to grab onto me."

Mina looked over her shoulder as Arthur yanked her out the door. She caught a glimpse of Blue across the room, still by the fireplace, and his eyes flashed a vibrant red for a split moment.

Mina blinked several times as Arthur forced her down the hallway. Had she really seen that? It wasn't possible. No one's eyes could change color like that. Could they?

Propelled forward by his grip, Arthur strode down one corridor and then another. He opened the door to an atrium and shoved her inside. Mina stumbled and pitched forward as the layers of material caught on her shoe. As she tumbled into an oversized potted plant, she worried she might rip her dress before showing it off.

As her hand landed in the soil, the scent of damp greenery and dirt invaded her. Anger rushed through her, heating her skin. She straightened and whipped around to face him, wiping her hands together as the doors closed, muting out the sounds of the party down the hall.

"How dare you."

"How dare I?" He strode forward. "You left without a word. Without a note. We had no idea where you'd gone. If you were dead."

"You think I don't know why you are really upset? It's because you knew that if I disappeared, you'd have no way to access the money before Father got home. You weren't worried about me. You were worried about yourself."

The words poured out of her unhindered. Words she'd never spoken before. Feelings deep inside that she would no longer hold at bay.

Arthur advanced on her and yanked the small clutch from her trembling hands. He ripped it open and tossed out her tissues and peppermint candies.

"Excuse you!"

He grabbed the stack of neatly folded bills and looked through them. "Is this all you brought with you? I need more."

"No, you don't. I paid the bill for the groceries and have a weekly delivery set up for food and supplies."

Arthur sneered and shoved the money in his pocket before tossing her purse.

"Well, you did a fine job these last few days, only being worried about yourself. Fancy new dress. Hair done. I assume you stayed in a hotel and had all your meals prepared for you while we stayed home and ate gluey oats and water. Must have been nice to be waited on hand and foot for a few days."

"You mean how I do for you, Quincey, and Lucy?" She stepped up to him. "Yes, I bought a dress. Father told me to. And I bought shoes too because Lucy's feet are a size smaller than mine and all her hand-me-downs kill my feet while I stand washing your clothes, preparing your meals, and cleaning the house. Tell me, Arthur, when was the last time you did anything for anyone but yourself? When was the last time you even gave me a thank you for everything I've done to keep our family together?"

"I don't need to thank you. That's your job, and your mother's before you," he spat.

Mina gasped. *Her* mother's?

Arthur snorted. "Didn't you ever wonder why you look so different from the rest of us?"

She shook her head. "You're lying."

"Ask Lucy and Quincey. Our mother was a woman of substance and stature. She died when Quincey was seven. Father couldn't handle his grief and fell prey to your mother's alluring smiles and lingering stares."

He was lying. It couldn't be. They all had the same mother. She advanced on him. "You're a liar! Father would have told me. You're just trying to hurt me because Father loves me more than you."

Arthur laughed. "He doesn't love you more. He treats you like a pet. He dotes on you and keeps you close, why? Because he's ashamed of you. Afraid others will discover the truth about who your mother was, he'll be ruined."

Mina shook her head. Her father did love her. "It's not true."

"Little Labrador retriever Mina. Like the one I used to have as a child. The one who used to lick my hand after I'd whipped him."

"Stop."

"You're just the same as that dog. Always so helpful. Never doing anything wrong. You know why we don't help out around the house? Because you are so damn easy to kick around. Just like my dog. So scared of his own shadow he didn't dare disobey me."

"Enough."

"And the day he did—"

"Shut up! Shut up! I am not a pet!" She slapped him.

Arthur's eyes flashed like her father's did every time he was ready for a fight, and before she could move, his fist raised in the air and swung toward her. She closed her eyes, waiting for the strike, but it didn't come. A crash sounded a few feet away, and she opened her eyes to find Blue standing by her and Arthur on his rear, covered in dirt from an overturned potted begonia.

Blue turned to her, his eyes like hard glass. "Are you all right?"

She nodded, unable to speak. Her blood rushed through her veins, but she hadn't been scared.

"My Lord." Arthur got to his feet. "My sister and I were just having a conversation. I was attempting to ascertain where she's been. Wasn't I, Mina?"

Mina looked between them. "Yes. Arthur was trying to figure out where I've been. And then he accused me of being selfish, and when I said something he didn't like, he decided striking me was the only way to show his displeasure."

"Get out of my house," said Blue.

"My Lord—"

Blue advanced on Arthur so fast that Mina didn't see him move. He grabbed Arthur by the throat and pulled him close.

"Leave my house." His voice came out so low Mina barely heard it.

"I'll just collect my sisters and—"

"You will leave my house alone."

Arthur shoved Blue's hand from his throat. "Not without my brother and my sisters. Sir. My father insisted we come together. Which means we leave together as well."

Blue turned to Mina. "Do you want to go home with your brother?"

This was the moment. If she stood up to Arthur now, there was no going home for her until her

father's return. And if she couldn't return home...
where would she go?

It didn't matter. The streets of London would be
safer for her at that moment than going home with
her siblings.

Mina swallowed hard. "No."

"Great. One down. Two to go."

The atrium door opened, and Renfield entered as
if silently beckoned.

"Sir, do you need my assistance?"

"Please get the remaining Murray siblings and
bring them here."

Renfield bowed and exited without a word. The
trio stood for several tense minutes until the door
opened again, and Lucy and Quincey arrived. Lucy
stopped at the sight of her, and her smile fell, but just
as quickly, the smile plastered back on her face.

"Mina, there you are. We were so worried." Lucy
rushed forward, but Blue stepped in her way, pushing
Arthur toward her. Arthur wobbled but caught himself.
He turned his enraged yet scared gaze on Blue.

"Your brother Arthur has overstayed his welcome.
He said he isn't leaving without his siblings. Therefore
I am giving you a choice. Stay or go with him."

Lucy's gaze moved to Arthur. "Arthur?"

"We're leaving." He marched toward the door
with Quincey, but Lucy stayed put, her gaze on Blue.

"Lucy, I said we are leaving," Arthur commanded.

She turned to Arthur. "I think I'd like to stay a bit longer."

Arthur opened his mouth and then shut it. "Fine. But you'll be the one to deal with Father when he finds out."

Mina's brothers exited, and Blue turned back to her. "He didn't hurt you, did he?"

Embarrassment flushed her skin. "No. Thank you."

Blue traced his fingers down her arm. "If he'd done anything to hurt you…"

"He didn't."

"And he never will."

"Yes." Lucy moved forward. "We would never let anything happen to you. Arthur can be so mean sometimes. Even I have been a victim of his temper before."

Blue gave Lucy a mild smile, like an impatient parent placating a troublesome child. "Lucy, I would hate for you to be away from your friends for too long. You are welcome to rejoin the other guests. Mina and I will be along presently."

"Oh…" She looked to Mina as if waiting for her to reject the idea, but Mina stayed silent. "All right then. I'll wait for you in the ballroom. I'll be sure to save the next dance for you."

Blue nodded. "Please, don't. I know there are at least a dozen young men in there who are pining to dance with you. I would hate for you to offend them on my behalf."

Lucy threw on a smile and headed for the door, glancing over her shoulder several times. Mina thought she might stop and say something, but in the end, she didn't.

"I'm sorry for my family," Mina said.

Blue gave her a tight smile. "Family can be tough."

Mina looked down at her dress and tried to brush the dirt from where it stained the silk. Her gaze went to the door, and she caught Lucy's red train disappearing out of sight.

"I will have your dress cleaned first thing in the morning."

"You are too kind. You don't need to do that."

"I insist. My maid, Iona, is amazing at removing stains much more noticeable than that small dirt smudge."

"That gown really does look amazing on Lucy." She sighed. "She's so much better at this than I am. Always has been. I supposed having fancy things is not what I am destined for."

"It was meant for you."

Mina chuckled. "No. I'm quite sure it was meant for Lucy. As you mentioned, she has many admirers."

"That may be, but I know for a fact that gown was not meant for her. I sent a card along with it. Surely, she got it and knew that as well."

Mina's cheeks flushed with heat. "You... sent the red dress?"

He stepped closer to her. "I saw it in London the day before and knew it would be perfect for you." He looked her up and down. "Jewel tones are your colors. If I'd seen this green one when I was there, I'd have had a hard time deciding. The red matches your lips, but this green matches your eyes."

"But... when did you have time to go to London? We'd only just seen you the evening before."

A mix of emotions crossed Blue's face.

"I'm sorry. I didn't mean to pry. That's none of my business."

Blue slipped his hand in hers. "You look ravishing in that dress."

"And you look quite magnificent in that suit."

Mina had so many things she wanted to say to him. So many questions she wanted to ask. At that moment, though, none came out of her mouth. What she said was, "Why is it when I'm with you, I feel like I could tell you anything? Like we've known each other for centuries?"

He brushed a hair from her forehead. "Maybe we have. Maybe in a past life. Or possibly two."

"You believe in reincarnation?"

"Who knows?"

She wanted to reach up and stroke his beard. To feel the thick, soft hairs between her fingers. But she dared not be so forward. "You promised you'd tell me your name."

He nodded. "And you promised you'd tell me yours."

"My father used to call me Mina. He said, my mother..." Her chest squeezed. Her mother. Who was her mother?

"What is it?"

She shook her head. "Just something Arthur said. That my mother wasn't his mother. That she was someone else."

"Is it possible?"

"I... I don't know. He was angry and in need of money like always, probably to cover his gambling debts." She sighed. "He could have been trying to be mean, but something in how he said it..."

"But if your mother and his mother were different women, don't you think you would have found out before now?"

"I honestly don't know what to believe. I used to think my siblings cared about me, and now I believe they only care about themselves. If I were honest, I'd say it made sense if my mother was someone else. It would explain much about their behavior toward me my whole life."

"It's hard to believe anyone could treat such a kind person so poorly just for who their parents were."

She chuckled. "Have you met the people in the ballroom yet? All they do is judge others for who their

parents are. Or their grandparents. Though surprisingly, not one of them had let it slip before now that
my father might have had an affair with a maid. Not
that I've ever associated with any of them outside of
my father or brothers or Lucy being there. So...
maybe it is possible."

"It sounds like you haven't gotten much time to
yourself in recent years. How did you enjoy your time
alone in London?"

Should she be honest with him? Why should she
not? She had been so far. "I must admit it was a bit
lonely after the museum."

His eyes glittered brighter, and he squeezed her
hand. "That is good to know."

"You want me to be lonely?"

"No, but it's always nice to know when you've
been missed."

He stepped toward her, but Mina wasn't sure what
she wanted. She walked to a nearby rosebush and
smelled a vibrant white rose. "What about you? Do
you have siblings?"

"I... did. A sister. She died a long time ago."

"And your parents?" She looked at him and
smelled another rose.

"Wonderful people. They, too, are long since
buried."

Mina frowned and turned toward him. "I'm sorry
to hear that. It must be hard."

He gave her a sad smile. "You have no idea. But

enough about that. Will you join me in the other room? I would love to dance with you."

He held out his arm to her. Mina hesitated. Part of her enjoyed their game—the back-and-forth, the seductive flirtations—but another part told her she was moving too fast. Jonathan's warning floated back to her.

She stared at his arm. "I have to admit, I never was very good at dancing. It's Lucy who has always been the better dancer."

"Why don't you let me be the judge?"

She shook her head. "I don't want to embarrass you at your party."

Blue caught her hand as she stepped away. "My dear, you could step on my feet all night. Stumble. Trip. Cause me to fall. And yet, still, I wouldn't be even one ounce embarrassed for it. To be embarrassed would imply that I care what the people out there think. And the only person whose opinion I care about is in this room with me."

Mina looked at his fingers joined lightly with hers and wondered when he'd taken her hand.

With every passing moment in his presence, she found herself falling a little bit more in love with Blue.

BLUE SAW NO ONE BUT MINA AS HE WHIRLED HER around the dance floor. Just as he'd suspected, she wasn't a bad dancer. It only made him believe even further that her siblings had heaped upon her nothing but mental abuse for the entirety of her lifetime. He could only assume their jealousy over her father's obvious affection caused them to treat her horribly. And now, to hear that she wasn't even born of the same mother, it made much more sense.

Blue heard every whisper of the guests. Caught every chuckle, every sideways glance, every remark made in hushed tones about Mina and his dancing together. Part of him wanted to rip out every tongue and drain those who dared to speak ill of such a radiant spirit. But the more sensible part of him knew the horrors that would follow if he did. There had been a time when he had bathed in blood. His life consumed with feeding and taking and killing. But after a century of leaving bodies in his wake, he'd found that blood only begat more blood, and surrounded by nothing but nameless bodies, he'd wished for nothing more than a companion to cherish and take care of.

It had taken him five hundred years and several mistakes to finally find the one. His one. The one he could share the rest of his eternity with. The only problem was... she was human, and he wanted her to stay that way.

.   .   .

They danced for close to an hour before Mina requested a break. Blue escorted her out onto the balcony overlooking the gardens and lands beyond.

They stood at the railing, and she lifted her chin toward the sky and drank in the moonlight. Her long, slender neck pulsed with life. Blue's fangs ached as he looked at her, wanting her, needing her.

"What brought you to England," she asked.

"I wanted a change of scenery. Where I'm from, everything seemed to have a bleak haze over it. After living there as long as I had, that haze began to seep into my soul. So I decided to move."

She laughed, a soft, tinkling sound that made him smile. "If only we all had it that easy. To just pick up and move wherever we want, whenever we want."

Blue's chest squeezed. "You could, you know. Go where you want, when you want." He moved closer and set his hand on top of hers. "I would take you anywhere your heart desired."

The sound of her pulse quickened in his ears. She looked to where his hand sat on hers, and the warmth of her skin heated beneath his fingers. She was the only one who had never pulled away from his icy touch. Never mentioned it. Never questioned, only accepted. She peered into his face, and her skin flushed a beautiful shade of peony.

"I... want to say that I would like that very much."

Blue closed the distance between them and

stroked the back of her hand with his thumb. "Then say it."

She looked at their hands again. "To say such a thing would be presumptuous and forward."

"But would it be a lie?"

She swallowed, and her voice barely came out a whisper. "No."

Blue's arm encircled her waist, and he turned her to face him. Her green eyes stayed on his chest, and he gently lifted her chin. He ran his knuckles across her cheek and still she didn't cringe. He wanted to kiss her. A long, passionate meeting of lips that simulated the pleasure he wanted to drench her body in.

"What's your name?" she asked.

"I want to kiss you, Mina."

She smiled. "Even better reason for you to tell me your name."

Blue moved in, letting his lips linger an inch from hers. He caught the taste of her warm breath in his mouth, and it took all his restraint to keep from unleashing his fangs and sinking them deep into her creamy throat. He nudged her forehead with his and then lay his cheek on hers.

"My name is Vladimir." He brushed his mouth against hers.

"Vlad... I like it better than Blue. It's a strong name. It suits you..." She licked her lips.

"May I kiss you?" he begged.

Her breath hitched. "Yes."

Blue urged her closer until her heartbeat echoed inside his chest. His mouth brushed hers again, and her lips parted slightly. Every fiber of him wanted her with an icy dragon fever.

"Mina?" Lucy's voice came out a mix of a shriek and a yell.

Mina backed out of his grip, and Blue fought the growl that rose in his throat.

"It's time to leave." Lucy stomped toward them and grabbed Mina by the arm.

"But—"

Lucy dragged her toward the open doors where, inside, the guests gawked at them.

"Lucy, stop." Mina tried picking up her hem so she didn't trip.

"We are leaving, and you better believe I am going to write to Father and make sure he knows exactly what kind of man has moved in next to us, trying to take advantage of a poor, naïve girl."

Blue opened his mouth to protest, but at that moment, Mina stopped moving.

"No." Mina's voice came out stronger than he'd ever heard. "You're just jealous because you thought he wanted you when he really wants me."

Lucy glanced around at the guests before donning her most sympathetic smile. "Don't be ridiculous. I am looking out for you and your well-being. He saw you there all timid and sweet and decided to take advantage. I will not allow you to be ruined by such a rogue."

Lucy reached for her again. Part of Blue wanted to rush to her side and protect her, but he couldn't. She needed to do this on her own. To show her sister and herself that she could stand on her own feet like he knew she could.

"Mina, you're acting like a child. Stop embarrassing yourself and come along."

Mina squared her shoulders. "It's you who are embarrassing yourself. And in my gown, no less."

Lucy's cheeks heated, and she scanned the now-gathering crowd. "I don't know what you—"

"That dress was meant for me, and you know it. Blue bought it for me, but you took it for yourself. That's all you do. All of you. Arthur, Quincey, you. You take and take and take. I'm tired of giving. Tired of cooking, cleaning, and being treated like a maid. But that's what I am, isn't it? My mother, she isn't your mother, is she? Was she the housemaid?"

Lucy's mouth opened and closed several times. Her eyes bulged, and then, as if a switch had flicked, her expression changed, and she smiled and then gave a practiced titter of laughter.

"Of course not. You know Arthur was being playful. Of course, we have the same mother. Father is an honorable man. He would never..." Her voice trailed off. Blue wasn't sure if she was lying to save her father's reputation or her own, but he was convinced it wasn't to help Mina.

Blue took the opportunity to join Mina. Placing his hand on her lower spine he smiled at the gathered group.

"I think it is time to call it a night," he announced. "All of this excitement has been quite enough for everyone. If you head toward the door, Renfield will be sure to get you your things. Thank you for joining us tonight. I look forward to seeing you again."

Renfield broke through the crowd when no one moved, ushering people out the door.

Lucy returned to where Mina stood, keeping her voice low. "If you do not come home with me now, I will—"

"Will what? What will you do? Tell father? Throw out my things? Never allow me to return? Be very careful how you answer. Remember, it is I that father left in charge, and whether or not you three eat this next month is very much in my hands."

Lucy sucked in a deep breath and then looked at Blue. Hatred seethed off her like a skunk stink. "Fine. Stay here. Spread your legs for him and prove yourself the same low-class, money-grubbing whore that your mother was. It's your grave that you dig. I will have no part of it."

Lucy headed for the door.

"Lucy?" Mina called.

Lucy turned.

"I'll have Jonathan come around later to collect my dress. Please see that you don't damage it before you get home and take it off."

Lucy's gaze turned vengeful as she stomped away.

Mina didn't move for a long minute, then suddenly, she tipped sideways. Blue caught her.

"I... I'm sorry." Her voice quavered.

He lifted her into his arms and whisked her into the house and upstairs to a room down the hall from his. He opened the door and set her on the side of the bed. She sat for several minutes, chest heaving, tears dripping onto the floor. Blue didn't speak. He simply allowed her to squeeze his hand in the moment of pain.

She swiped at the tears in her eyes. "I warned you that I would embarrass you."

"And I told you I don't care what those people think." He chuckled. "What can I do to help?"

She looked at him, and he wiped a tear from her cheek. "Nothing. You've been too kind to me already. I should go."

She stood, and a streak of panic rushed through him. "Where?"

She sniffled and blotted her eyes again. "I don't know. Back to London, I suppose."

"Yes, but there are no more trains for tonight."

She shrugged. "I..."

"Stay here," he blurted. "I have plenty of room.

You can choose any you'd like. Stay and gather your thoughts. Decide tomorrow what you want to do."

"I can't possibly. It wouldn't be proper."

"And sleeping out in the woods would be? Something tells me that would be your solution, and you could freeze to death. That dress is beautiful but not at all practical for this weather. Please. I promise to be a complete gentleman."

"All you've been is a gentleman. I wouldn't now expect you to be anything otherwise."

Blue touched her cheek. So sweet. So mild. And yet she'd shown such incredible strength and resilience in the face of such horrible betrayal by her siblings.

"I'll send in one of the maids to help you out of your clothes."

She shook her head. "That's not necessary."

Blue kissed her hand and bowed before moving reluctantly for the door. "You are welcome here as long as you'd like."

"Vlad?"

He froze at the sound of his name. No one had called him that in so long... no other woman had ever been told his name. His mother had taught him that names held power, and he finally understood her words. His name on Mina's lips had him ready to obey her every request.

"Yes, my dear?"

"I can never repay your kindness."

His body ached to go to her and spread her beneath him, feeling her warm flesh under his.

"Your happiness is repayment enough." His fangs burst from his gums, and before she could say another word, he slipped out the door, ran down the hallway, dove out the open window, and flew into the night.

CHAPTER TEN

Mina tossed and turned for several hours and finally arose from the stiff bed that wasn't her own. Locating a shawl in the corner wardrobe, she wrapped it around herself. She looked out into the night sky and fought once more to keep tears from her eyes.

All those years, her father had never told her who her birth mother was. Had the wonderful stories he'd regaled her with about her mother's beauty, grace, and kindness been about her mother or his wife? He'd obviously sworn her siblings to silence, but who else had been privy to the secret all this time? Who had stared at her behind her back, shaking their head and whispering about how pitiful it was that she didn't know the truth? Or worse yet, had laughed or mocked or made fun of her? Probably everyone. And now, finally, she knew the truth, but not who she was.

The view outside the bedroom window was different from the view she'd grown up with in her room. Blue's vast and angular garden wasn't unlikable. The hedges were trimmed relatively short and efficiently. Tiny boxwoods, if she remembered correctly.

A group of shadows raced through the back of the green, followed closely by a white blur. Mina lay her hand against the glass, trying to get a better look. Wolves. They had to be the wolves she'd seen on her own estate. But... she hadn't remembered there being a white wolf with them. A white wolf like—she stopped at the thought. It couldn't possibly be the wolf from London.

Mina staggered from the window as a chill skittered over her body. She remembered how the wolf had bent to Blue's gaze, calming itself. And now to see a white wolf running across Blue's lands... wolves that hadn't been seen in England for hundreds of years... She bumped into a small table and turned in time to catch a statue as it teetered on the edge, ready to crash to the floor.

She sucked in a sharp breath, setting it back in its spot. She wrapped the shawl around herself tighter and examined the room. Melancholy-colored walls pressed inward around her. Ghostly thin curtains billowed from the crack in the window pane. The ceiling creaked above her, and the house groaned against the strong wind. The musty, woodsy smells of

Blue's estate were so different from the warm wooden scents of her home. And the room temperature ran at least ten degrees cooler, even with the fires burning.

The air hummed through the structure and had a taste she couldn't quite place. Aside from the statue on the small table, there were no small adornments in the room, no frills, nothing to invite someone in and make them feel comfortable. Everything about the space was... not home. It had been different in the hotel, but it was supposed to be—it was a hotel. But in Blue's house, it felt so strange—comfortable despite its oddness.

Mmmmmiiiiiiinnnnnaaaaaa.

She whipped around at the whispered hiss of her name, but no one was there.

She waited... holding her breath...

Again, her name hissed through her mind so faintly that she couldn't tell if she'd imagined it.

As if lulled by a soothing command, she crossed to the door and cracked it open.

Whispers floated toward her, encompassing her mind and tempting her forward.

"Hello... Blue?"

The tinkle of a woman's laughter made her skin pebble.

"Lucy?" she whispered. "Lucy, is that you?"

A soft humming floated from the floor below. Mina looked around and grabbed a candelabra from a table in the hall. She passed several rooms to the sizable red-carpeted staircase and descended on tiptoe.

"Mmmmiiiiiiinnnaaaa. Where are you?" a voice beckoned.

She followed the sound down the stairs and around toward the right. The air surrounding her grew frosty as she headed for an ornate arched door. Her heartbeat reverberated in her ears like the strike of a blacksmith's hammer, and with each step she took, her limbs grew heavier and more sluggish. She reached Blue's study and stared at the door. She vaguely remembered sneaking into the room when she was young with her friend Gretchen. They'd giggled as they'd gone through Gretchen's father's desk, looking for coins to toss into the fountain in the garden.

She reached for the doorknob; her fingers outstretched for several seconds before she let her palm land on the cool metal. She tried to twist it. It didn't move. Locked.

Mina pulled her fingers away, shaking her head and looking around. What was she doing? What if someone saw her? Blue would think she was snooping. That was not the way to repay the man who had done so much for her.

Mina backed away from the door and headed for the stairs. Fatigue. It had to be the fatigue and the events of the previous evening that had caused her to go down there. She needed to get right back upstairs and get some sleep. She crept up two steps before a slow click sounded, and the previously locked door creaked open.

Mina turned. A sliver of light inched out the small opening. She stared at it for a good long minute. It was her imagination. It had to be. It hadn't been locked before. She'd only thought it was.

Mina listened to the sounds of the house for a moment. If she left the door open, Blue would know someone had tried to enter. She had to close it. Dashing back down the stairs to the door, she reached for the knob.

Mmmiiiiiiinnnaaaaaa.

She stopped.

Mmmmiiiiiiinnnaaaaaa. Come and play.

"No," she whispered. "It's just in your head. You are tired. You need to rest."

The door swung inward a couple inches. Someone was toying with her. Had someone from the party stayed behind? If so, they wouldn't like the response they were about to receive.

Unable to hold back her curiosity, Mina pushed the door open.

"Who's in here?"

She looked around the ornate study. Books lined one wall from floor to ceiling, and a resplendent fireplace took up most of another. Part of her wished to run her fingers over the books and pick one for herself, but the enormous tapestry above the fireplace caught her attention. A man with bluish-black hair rode an equally dark stallion into battle. On his blood-stained shield was the symbol of a dragon. Under the stallion lay a thousand dead bodies. Behind, several towns stood in flames.

Mina swallowed hard as she looked up into the bright eyes of the man on the steed. *Blue.*

She inched closer to the tapestry and lifted the candelabra to inspect the portrait better. Bloodstained Blue's entire uniform. His horse's feet were soaked, and even Blue's mouth and face were splattered. His lips twisted into a triumphant grin as he held a banner high above his head with the same dragon symbol as his shield.

Mina's hand shook at the sight of the carnage. Fear and excitement roiled around inside her as they always did when she witnessed such violence. Seeing him upon his horse, Mina felt more drawn to Blue than ever. The thrill of a man wielding such power, even if it was just in a portrait, made her shiver with desire.

A small sound, like that of a wounded animal, came from inside the fireplace. Mina moved closer, and the whimpering grew louder. She stepped into the hearth and lifted the candles upward to see if something had gotten stuck in the chimney, but all she saw was blackness.

She went to step out of the fireplace when she heard the noise again. Pressing her ear to the stone, she listened. From behind the fireplace came a scratching, whimpering sound.

"Hell... Hello?"

Help us, Mmiiiinnaaaa.

Mina stumbled backward.

"Mina!"

She turned, dropping the candelabra. Blue rushed forward, his expression frantic. He picked up the flaming candles and stomped out the sparks. With a bang, he set the candelabra on his desk and crossed to her.

"What are you doing in here?"

She took a step away from him at the frantic expression on his face. "I... I heard a voice..." She looked at the fireplace. "And—"

"Mina. Where did you get the key for my study?"

She looked over his shoulder. "The door was unlocked."

Blue took her by the arms and made her face him. Something inside told her to run from him- that Blue was dangerous. Close up she noticed a fine sheen of sweat covered his face. Though he'd been in bed, he smelled of the woods and dirt. How was that possible?

"Mina."

His gaze intensified and she found she couldn't look away. Every muscle in her body turned and focused on him. His face loomed ever closer to hers and his eyes seemed to enlarge until nothing else filled her vision but the deep blue of his irises.

"Mina, you are never to come in this room. Never. You can go anywhere else in the house you want but never *this* room. Do you understand?" His voice reverberated around the room. The hushed whisper of "Never enter" ricocheted off the walls, shelves, and books, winding around her and nuzzling their way into her mind.

All fear and doubt fell away, and she wanted nothing more than to please him and bend to his will. It felt like the most natural request in the world. Of course, she would never come in his study again. It was his. His private space. She never should have invaded his privacy. It wasn't her right. She would stay out of his room no matter what.

"Of course, Blue."

Without warning, he took her in his arms and pressed her head into his chest. The sensation startled her but also warmed her at the same time. She shook her head, dazed.

"Come," he said. "You need to rest."

She nodded. "I need to rest."

Mina walked with his arm around her shoulders as he ushered her back to her room. She tried to focus, but her head felt like someone had filled it with cotton. She looked over her shoulder. She could have sworn she'd heard voices in the fireplace, but that was silly. Why would there be people in the fireplace? She'd been ridiculous to think so. She was just glad Blue wasn't angry with her for having been so absurd.

It was good that he'd come along and stopped her from doing anything too foolish.

Swiftly, he helped her back up the stairs and down the hallway. A warning nagged at the back of her mind. A warning she couldn't quite place, but a hint that told her she was somehow still in danger.

Blue opened the door, and she faced him, suddenly exhausted. He pushed her hair over her shoulder and stared at her before yanking her into his arms again.

"I'm sorry I had to do that," he whispered so softly she barely caught it. "It's for your own good."

He kissed her forehead and smiled as he walked her to the bed, tucked her in, and then strode out of the room without another word.

Her eyelids opened and closed slowly as if the very movement weighed her down. As her eyes closed, one foggy thought floated through her head repeatedly as she drifted to sleep.

What was he sorry for?

"THE STUDY WAS LOCKED. I CHECKED IT MYSELF AFTER you departed." Renfield walked with Blue into his room.

"Then how did she get in?" he demanded.

"She said she heard voices coming from behind the fireplace."

Blue shook his head. "*Fecior de curva.*" He punched the wall, making the stone shake and dust rain down on him. *"Get an extra lock on the door first thing in the morning."*

"Do you think a lock is going to fix the problem?"

Blue stared hard, but as always, Renfield didn't even flinch. "You don't approve of her being here."

"It doesn't matter whether or not I approve. I am here to keep you safe, as I have done for generations. And that means keeping your secrets. Having her here puts you in jeopardy. The party tonight was reckless. Going to London to feed is also not ideal, but it's better than feeding here in the country. Most concerning, from what I've seen tonight, is that her family will not let Mina go. If you want her, which it's obvious you do, you should go. Marry and take her as far away from her family as possible."

Renfield wasn't wrong. "And what about the others?"

Renfield didn't blink. "As I said, I've been caring for you and your family for generations. I will do what is necessary to keep doing that."

Get Mina away not only from her family but from his as well.

Blue's gaze traveled to the stairs.

MARRIS HISSED AS BLUE SLAMMED HER INTO THE wall.

"What do you think you're doing?" he demanded.

She squirmed in his grasp, her fangs snapping together. "I just wanted to see her."

Blue pulled her from the wall and slammed her into it again, making her silver chains clatter on the floor.

"You stay the hell away from Mina, understand?" He squeezed her throat. She grabbed onto his arm and scratched at him with her talons. "You stay away from her body and out of her mind."

"We just wanted to see her," she choked out.

Blue pulled her close. "You don't see her. You don't hear her. You don't smell her. If you try to call to her again, I'll take you into the garden, stake you to the grass, and let the sunlight take you."

"What does she have that I don't?" Marris crooned, running her fingers up Blue's arm. "We used to be so close. Remember our nights bathing in blood, feeding together, sharing everything? We could do that again."

Blue's fangs dropped into his mouth. Memories of who he used to be flooded him. *Beds of blood. Bodies piled high. Making love all night.*

Marris moved in close, her lips almost touching his. "We could have that, Blue. You could have me."

Blue's gaze focused on her again, and he threw her to the floor. She hissed and scrambled away.

"You are no more tempting to me, witch, than a dolled-up swine."

Marris screamed at him, and Blue rolled down his sleeves. He scanned the small, stone room. "You are lucky I've let you live. I could have killed you, like Suzetta."

"Live?" Marris screeched. "You call this living? Feeding us animal blood. Keeping us in chains?"

"If you don't like it here, I can make other arrangements. Trust me, it would be much easier on me if I let you die."

"You'd like that, wouldn't you? So you could erase your past and move on with your newest little sweetie. But she'll end up like the rest of us. She and I will meet sooner or later."

Blue wanted to strike her for her words. To yell at her and tell her Mina would never turn out like them. Mina was his soulmate. She would never be like the rest. Instead, he turned and headed through the fireplace to his study beyond. He closed the secret wall and ran his fingers through his hair.

He couldn't chance there being another incident with Mina. He wouldn't risk anything happening to her. He had to tell her the truth about what he was, but if he told her now, she might run back to her family. And they were more likely to kill her than anyone in his house. He needed to get her away. The question was, how?

CHAPTER ELEVEN

Draugr

Mina awoke the next morning to find the box with the red gown sitting on the chair beside her bed. Her stomach clenched at the thought of Jonathan having to go over and get it from Lucy. She imagined that hadn't been a pleasant experience for him. She assumed Blue had asked him to do it since she'd not gotten the opportunity.

She noticed a bag beside the chair and sat up to discover her father's old military suitcase on the floor. She opened it and found some dresses and under-things shoved inside. Had Lucy packed it as a kind-ness, hoping Mina wouldn't return? Or as a final farewell? She really couldn't be sure.

Mina swallowed her guilt at leaving her siblings to fend for themselves. No matter how they felt about her, it wasn't right. She refused to be as spiteful as they were.

A sense of foreboding overcame her as she tried to play the previous night's events in her head. After the party and going to bed, she vaguely recalled getting up and going downstairs because she'd heard voices. But she couldn't clearly remember going back to bed. She got the vague sense that something had happened and Blue had brought her back to her room, but the memory was fuzzy around the edges, like it had been a dream. The idea made her shiver. It was just like when she'd been at the museum with him.

An ominous sense overtook her. She didn't like the holes that seemed to be forming in her memories. She no longer believed that an excess of alcohol was the cause of her memory loss in the museum. Something was happening to her—something she wasn't okay with.

THIRTY MINUTES LATER, MINA OPENED HER DOOR. She looked down the dim hallway to the long line of rooms and wondered if any belonged to Blue. She pondered what he would look like in his bed. What did he wear? Her cheeks flushed at the thought. She shook her head and reminded herself that she could no longer trust him. Between her weird memory loss and Jonathan's warnings, she wasn't sure what to believe.

Mina headed for the stairs and descended to the lower level, listening for any sound. She stopped, and her gaze traveled to the closed study door. The overwhelming feeling to stay away from it passed through her. She stepped toward it and then turned right around as if spun by an invisible hand and walked toward the kitchen.

The closer she got, the louder voices floated toward her. She recognized Jonathan as one of them.

"I'm telling you something isn't right," Jonathan said. "Two locks on a man's study? He's hiding something."

"Maybe the man just likes his privacy, and now that Mina is here, he wants to make sure he gets it," a woman replied.

"That's silly. Mina isn't staying."

"Are you so sure about that?"

Mina entered the kitchen, and Jonathan looked up from his bowl.

"Are you all right?"

Mina gave him a tight smile as he crossed and hugged her. "Yes, I'm fine."

"I heard what happened last night as everyone was leaving. I tried to find you. When I heard the rumors that you'd stayed the night here, I raced to check on you, but Count Draugr said you were asleep." He shook his head. "First Arthur and then Lucy. It's all anyone is talking about. I can't believe they were so horrible. It was unforgivable. It's why I made Lucy pack some of your things for you and brought them back with me a little while ago."

Mina stepped out of his hug. "Thank you. You didn't have to do that."

She wanted to ask him if he'd known about her mother. If he'd been privy to it the whole time. But the compassion in his gaze made her think he hadn't known.

"It's the least of what you deserve. If I'd had enough gumption, I would have told her exactly what I thought of her. Arthur, as well."

"That's quite all right. You don't need to get into my family drama."

Jonathan snorted and squeezed her arm. "Has there ever been a time I haven't been?"

"Just the same. I want you to stay away from them. They're in a bad place right now."

"And you as well. At least until your father returns."

That was the plan.

He licked his lips and blinked several times. Mina knew that expression. He did it when he was nervous about talking to her about something.

"You are welcome to stay with Mother, Charlie, and me until your father returns."

"Are you hungry?" asked the cook. "I can make you something."

"Thank you." Mina sighed inwardly, grateful for

the interruption. "But I was hoping Jonathan could give me a ride to town."

"Are you going back to London? That could be good as well. Then I could visit you—"

"No. No." Mina's nerves began to fray like the edges of an overused blanket. She didn't know how much more she could take. "I just need to go to town, please. I need to go to the store to pay off our debt and make sure food delivery makes it to the house every week."

His eyebrows smashed together. "Then... where are you going to stay?"

"Uh..." Mina fiddled with her hair. "I am not sure. I'll have to speak to Blue—"

"Blue? You're on a first-name basis now?"

Mina glanced at the cook, who kept her gaze on the loaf of bread she was kneading. "Jonathan, Blue, and I are... friends."

"You barely know him."

"Even so, he helped me last night and offered me shelter. Before I make any decisions, I should speak to him."

Anger crossed Jonathan's face, and then he nodded. "I'll grab my coat and get the horses."

"There's no rush. You can finish your breakfast."

"Thank you, but I'm done. I have to go to town anyway to find a locksmith."

Mina's gut clenched. Jonathan's feelings were hurt because she wasn't turning to him. Unfortunately, though she appreciated his offer to let her stay with him, she and he would never be anything more than friends.

JONATHAN STOPPED THE CARRIAGE IN FRONT OF THE general store and opened the door for her.

"I won't be long."

He nodded but didn't meet her eye. "If I'm not here when you are done, I'll return shortly."

His formal tone tempted her to chastise him, but she didn't. A man with hurt pride wasn't one to be trifled with. Even Jonathan.

She placed her hand atop his. "Please don't be cross with me, Jonathan. I don't think I could bear it if another person I cared for were cross with me."

He looked down at her, and his eyes softened. "I'm sorry, Mina. But you have to know—"

"I do." She squeezed his hand. "And that's why I could never ask for a better brother than you. Even though you aren't truly my brother. You have been more of a friend to me than my siblings... half-siblings, I suppose."

He took a deep breath. "Then, as your friend and someone who loves you, please take my advice. Get out of that house. Go to London, where you will be safe."

"But why, Jonathan? Why do you think it's not safe there?" Though she wasn't sure she was safe herself, she needed to know what he had heard or seen. She needed something more to go on than just the ominous feeling that had been stalking her of late.

He looked around. "There's just something not right with the Count. He's adding extra locks to which only he and Renfield hold the keys. It sounds silly, but I know he's hiding something. There are the wolves and blood—"

"Blood?"

Jonathan shook his head. "I don't want to scare you. But I tell you, I think there is something sinister going on in that house. And I don't want you to get caught up in it."

Mina swallowed hard. Everything Jonathan believed sounded logical. And it aligned with the sense of foreboding she'd experienced that morning when she'd awoken. Even so, she couldn't deny her attraction to Blue or the feelings she held for him deep inside. Maybe it was the sense of danger that she felt in his arms. Perhaps it was his commanding presence. Or the way he, like her, didn't care much about what others thought. She didn't know. All she knew was that she felt tied to him in a way that both enthralled and scared her.

Mina looked up and down the street before heading to the store. The bell chimed as she entered the shop. She crossed to the counter. A woman and her daughter finished paying for their goods and turned to Mina. She smiled, and the woman gave her a tight smile before pulling her daughter away. The two whispered as they passed, and Mina swallowed hard, keeping her smile firmly planted on her face.

"Miss Mina, how are you today?" asked Mr. Giles.

"I am well, thank you."

"And what can I get for you?"

"I came in to pay off my family's bill and set up a weekly delivery for them."

"Well, that is a surprise—but a good surprise." He reached beneath the counter and pulled out his ledger. "Let's get you settled, and then I'll get your bracelet from my safe."

Mina nodded. "I'd appreciate that very much." Now more than ever, she wanted her bracelet. She was sure that it had been her birth mother's. It was the only thing she was sure of in her newfound situation.

Mina looked around the shop, and for several minutes, she let her thoughts get away from her as she felt the silk ribbons and lace that hung on a rack. She wondered what Blue would think of her in them. She dropped them and moved on. It was ridiculous to suddenly become the girl who wanted to get frilly for a man's attention, especially when she'd never been one before.

"Here it is." Mr. Giles walked back into the shop.

Mina smiled at the sight of her bracelet. "I can't thank you enough for your kindness."

"Kindness is given where kindness is received."

Mina placed the bracelet on her wrist. "I need a weekly delivery sent to the house for the next three weeks. I can pay in advance."

Mina opened her purse and pulled out enough money for the bill and the supply list she'd made.

"If you could arrange a delivery, I can pay extra."

He chuckled. "Never. I will make sure they are delivered, but I won't charge you anything more." He picked up the list. "I can have these delivered today."

"The day after tomorrow will be just fine." She didn't think leaving her siblings with what little was in the house was such a bad idea.

Mina passed over the money and spotted the jar of peppermints. "May I get a small bag of those as well?"

The shopkeeper smiled and nodded. The bell over the door rang as he got out the paper bag. Mina looked at the newcomers and swallowed hard as Octavia and Sera, her sister's best friends, entered the shop. Her stomach flopped, and she contemplated hiding from them, but what was the use? It couldn't have been a coincidence that they'd arrived at that moment. Especially when the last time she'd been in town, they'd insisted they'd never shop there again. Their arrival could only mean one thing: Mina and her family were the center of society gossip.

Mr. Giles handed over Mina's bag of candy as Octavia and Sera headed straight for her.

"Mina, darling." Octavia smiled. "How are you?"

"We were so worried," said Sera. "We heard Count Draugr might be keeping you prisoner."

Mina gave them a polite smile. "I'm afraid nothing half as worthy of gossip as that. Blue simply offered me a place to stay while my siblings and I work out a few problems."

Octavia stepped forward and squeezed Mina's hand, throwing a fake frown. "Yes, we heard Arthur told you. Terrible business for you to find out that way."

"Yes," Sera parroted. "Simply terrible. He had no right to do that. Your father should have been the one to tell you."

"Though I always thought your father should have told you years ago."

"You knew?" Mina asked.

Octavia gave her a sympathetic smile. "Lucy told us forever ago. We've all always felt so sorry for you."

Anger bubbled inside Mina. So everyone had known but her.

She straightened her shoulders. "Oh, you need not feel sorry for me. There's nothing to feel sorry for."

"Of course," said Sera. "What does it matter that your mother was the housemaid?"

"Lucy's mother had been dead for months by then. And your poor father, stricken with grief. Men have their needs, and they will have them tended to wherever they can, I'm afraid."

To keep from saying what she wanted to, Mina bit her tongue until pain shot through her head.

"Which is why we were concerned for you," said Octavia. "We just wanted to make sure that the Count hadn't tried to take any... liberties with you."

"I beg your pardon?"

"It's like Octavia said. Men have needs, and when he has a sweet, innocent young girl under his roof, who is to know what a man might do."

Both women nodded in unison.

Venom churned inside Mina like acid. She wanted to spew it all over the two stuck-up she-devils like a viper striking its prey, but to do so would do nothing but bring more shame upon herself and Blue.

"Blue has been kind and caring for me and my situation. I can promise you there is nothing nefarious about his intentions toward me. Now, if you will excuse me—"

Mina went to step around them, but Octavia caught her by the arm.

"Be careful, my dear, sweet Mina. We women must go so far as to keep ourselves from even the appearance of impropriety. I'd hate to see your reputation tarnished forever because of gossip about *Blue*."

Mina snorted. "Do you not think the rumors of my mother being a housemaid aren't enough to ruin me? Not that I care. I've never given a second thought to any of the people who seem so keenly interested in my history. And I'm sure that just as this

conversation will be the topic of every social engage-
ment *you* have for the next month, it will be
completely forgotten by *me* as soon as I step outside.
Good day."

Mina marched to the door, refusing to look back.
Instead, she headed straight to the carriage, stepped
inside, and stared ahead. So many things had
happened to her in the past weeks. Beginning with
almost getting run over by Blue's horses. Then, the
strange events with Blue in London. Next, her father
leaving, and the revelation that she wasn't who she
thought she was. Lastly, there was that weird whispering of her name and Blue's demand that she never
enter his study again.

Mina blinked rapidly at the sudden memory of
what had happened the night before. All of it accu-
mulated with everyone in town staring at her like she
was a leper, and she broke down. Sobs wracked her
body, and she sat back, hiding her face from a
prying eye.

Jonathan appeared in the window. "Where to?"

Mina sucked in a breath and blotted the tears
from her eyes. Where to? Where should she go? She
needed room and time to think. And she couldn't very
well go home. She blew out a cleansing breath. There
was only one other place she could go.

"Take me to the train station."

Jonathan hopped into the driver's seat and slapped
the reins on the horses. She needed to get out of

town. She needed to clear her head. She needed to decide what she was going to do.

Blue arose late that afternoon and smiled for the first time in a long time at the thought that Mina was in his house. He would have been made all the happier if she were in his arms, in his bed, locking lips with his, but he would be satisfied with merely having her in his proximity.

He prepared for the evening while attempting to find an excuse for leaving her alone all day. Yes, to say he had business was an excuse he had used in the past, but it wouldn't work with her, not for long. She was too intelligent not to question where he went and what he did all day.

A knock sounded on his door, and Blue opened it. Renfield waited.

"Was the lock taken care of?"

"Yes," said Renfield.

"Good. I've mulled it over, and I think I shall take your advice. I will ask Mina to accompany me to Spain. We will go by train and stay for at least several weeks. From there, I will explain to her what I am and—"

"She's gone."

A pain shot through his heart at the words, like

the stab of a silver dagger. As the words swirled in his mind, he barely got out his next question. "When?"

"Mr. Harker took her to the train station this morning after she attended to some business in town."

"Where did she go?" A hurricane of fear whipped around him and swirled his mind into a frenzy of terror.

Renfield shrugged. "I do not know."

Blue paced his room. Gone. She'd left him. Had it been his demand of her never to enter his study again? Or Marris? Or something else entirely?

"Pack my bag. I'm going to London."

"Maybe it's better this way. Maybe—"

Blue dropped his heated gaze on Renfield, who closed his mouth immediately.

"I'll pack your things."

"Pack for up to a month."

Blue turned to the window. Beyond the curtains, the sunlight deepened in hue, and the beam across the floor had grown shorter.

He had close to half an hour before the sun set completely. It was entirely too long for him to wait to go to London, but he needed to. And by taking a bag, he wouldn't be able to fly. If he were lucky, he'd get on the train and make it to London before midnight.

Who knew what kind of trouble she could get herself into by that time?

CHAPTER TWELVE

Mina wandered down the street, her mind on everything but her location. She'd spent hours pacing the city, trying to make sense of everything that had happened to her and, most importantly, Blue. She took corners without thinking and bypassed shops without seeing them while she analyzed his every word, every touch, every gesture.

She wasn't one to be taken in by a rake, and nothing in his behavior spoke of deceit. He knew she had no money, so there was no reason for him to be so kind to her in hopes of gaining control of her fortune. She wasn't a great beauty, so it wasn't like having her on his arm would boost other men's admiration. And she didn't hold a title, so he couldn't advance his position by being with her. She could not see him gaining one thing from starting a friendship with her. If anything, with the newest developments with her family, associating with her was more likely to tarnish his name than help. Yet every strange thing that had happened to her had happened with or because of Blue. And Jonathan's warnings were not without merit. Blue was a strange one indeed. And yet...

The sun had set when she finally looked up and discovered herself down by the docks. The salty breeze caressed her face, and the scent of fish and seaweed brought with it memories of inspecting her father's ships as a little girl. They were the times she'd seen her father the happiest.

Mina stared at the ships with their giant steam engines, and her thoughts traveled to her father. He'd not even been gone a whole week, and already everything had gone to hell. Sadly for her siblings, he would blame them for failing to maintain dignity. She wondered what would have happened if he'd never left. Would she ever have found out the truth about her mother? Would she even have been allowed to go to Blue's party? Surely, she never would have ended up in London spending time with him. Nor would she have ended up spending the night at Blue's estate. It amazed her how her father's iron gloves kept a tight hold on her and her life.

How she longed to board one of the ships and sail wherever it was headed without a thought for looking back, to disappear and become someone new. Someone not burdened by her past and the past of her family. But to leave would mean leaving Blue, and even though danger and mystery surrounded him like he was made of them, she couldn't deny her feelings for him. She at least owed him an opportunity to explain his strange behavior and why he'd demanded she never enter his study. And why, when she was with him, there were gaps in her memory. After all, maybe it wasn't Blue's fault. Possibly, there was something wrong with her. Could the stress of her family be causing her to lose her mind?

"Evening, Miss. Spare a few coins?"

Mina turned as a gaunt man in ragged clothes shuffled toward her. She stared at him blankly for a few moments before his question registered.

Mina removed her coin purse and opened it, looking for the change at the bottom. "Yes. Of course."

The man continued to amble forward as she caught several coins and held them out to him.

"Bless you, Miss." He drew closer, and she caught a glimpse of his eyes. His eyes were not those of a beggar's. Instead, they were alight and determined. He closed the distance between them, and Mina noticed his clothes weren't as shabby as she'd initially thought. They were merely smudged with soot and dirt, as was his face. A chill swept through her. Something was amiss.

Mina swallowed hard and dropped the coins to the ground. "I'm sorry." She backed away.

The man stepped over the coins, not even glancing at them. "What are you doing out here so late?"

"I... my father is an admiral, and I'm meeting him here."

A leering smile played on the man's lips as he continued to advance. "The last ship came in two hours ago."

Mina's chest pounded as her head told her to get away. "I must have missed him then. I'll just head home and meet him there."

"And where is it you live?"

"I..." Mina turned and ran. Her shoes clicked on the wooden planks as she hurried away. She didn't get far before a solid grip landed on her shoulder, yanking her to a stop.

Mina screamed, but a grease-smudged hand clamped over her mouth as warm alcohol-laden breath hit her neck.

"Don't do that." Something sharp pressed to her throat, and she felt the tingle of her skin splitting. "I'll slit your throat if you scream again."

Mina fought the panic that threatened to have her unleashing another scream as a trickle of blood dripped down between her breasts.

"Now." The man's hand left her mouth and moved down her throat and over her breasts to her waist. "You and I are going to go somewhere nice and quiet to get to know each other. And if you treat me right, I'll let you live. Do you understand?"

Mina nodded, but her mind raced. She couldn't allow him to take her anywhere. If she did, she was as good as dead.

The man removed the knife from her throat and pushed her forward. "Let's go."

Mina pitched forward, pretending to trip. If he were going to do something to her, he'd have to do it in the open. Her hands hit the dock, sending a shooting pain up her arms. She braced herself for whatever would come next, but nothing did. She waited, the sound of her harsh breathing pounding in her ears. A faint gurgling sound emanated behind her, and she squeezed her eye shut. Moments passed, and still, nothing happened. Finally, breathing, she turned to see a man striding toward her. He bent close and offered her his hand.

"Mina."

Relief mixed with fear as Blue's face swam into view, and he helped her to her feet.

"You shouldn't be here." He moved her forward.

"Where... where's that man?"

Blue continued to usher her off the dock. "What, man?"

"The man who attacked me." She looked over her shoulder, but Blue propelled her forward.

"I don't know what you mean."

Mina planted her feet and pulled away from him. "There was a man. He attacked me."

Blue walked closer, his eyes locking on hers. "Mina—"

"Stop!" She shut her eyes. "Stop treating me like a child. And don't do whatever it is you do that makes me feel light-headed and not fully remember things. I know you did something at the museum and then at your house. I don't know how, and I don't know what, but you did, didn't you?"

Silence stretched out for a long minute.

"Yes," he whispered.

Mina opened her eyes and looked at him. Fear and anxiety coursed over his face.

"What did you do?"

"I compelled you."

"What does that mean?"

Blue didn't move a muscle. "It means I forced you to bend to my will."

"Why would you do that?"

"In the museum, I didn't mean to. I just wanted to be close to you. To feel you. Touch you. I wasn't sure you'd let me. It's the same as when you walked into the party. But last night... I did it because I was scared and trying to keep you safe."

The truth rang through in his words, though she didn't quite understand how he'd done it.

"Are you a hypnotist?"

"Not exactly."

"And what about the man who attacked me? Where is he?" she demanded.

"Mina—"

"Where?" She stopped short of stamping her foot. She'd just told him to stop treating her like a child. It would do her no good to act like one.

Blue searched her face for a moment and then sighed. His shoulders slumped. He took her by the hand and led her around a stack of palates several yards away.

She looked down at the body on the ground. The man's very own knife protruded from his chest, and his eyes stared blankly upward. An odd sensation overcame her. Without thinking, she dropped to her knees, grabbed the knife, and ripped it from his chest. Then she plunged it into him again. And again. And again. She wasn't sure how many times she stabbed him, but eventually, Blue pulled her to her feet and cradled her close. She breathed deeply, but no tears fell.

She was done with people taking advantage of her. Of people thinking her weak. Of people thinking they could treat her as their personal toy to beat or use up and throw away. She was done being a victim of others' sick games.

She pressed away from Blue and looked him straight in the eye. His face remained passive as he pulled a handkerchief from his pocket and wiped blood from her face and throat.

"How did you know where I was tonight?" Her voice came out calmer than she'd anticipated.

"I..."

"Don't lie. If you ever want to see me again, don't lie."

Blue's gaze connected with hers as he continued to wipe away the dead man's blood. "Jonathan confessed he'd dropped you at the station. I assumed London was where you would go."

"But London isn't small."

"I... heard you scream after I checked into the hotel."

"That's miles from here."

"And yet, I heard you."

She grabbed his hand, and he stopped wiping. He could compel her. Throw her brother across a room, breaking a potted plant. Move quicker than she could see. Hear her scream from miles away.

"What are you?"

He encircled her waist with his free arm. "I do not age. I do not change. My heart no longer beats like a human's. I am immortal."

"A god?"

"Not even by half. In Romania, we are known as Strigoi, Varcolac, Vampir."

"Vampire?" Her body trembled, and she fought to process the word. A minute passed. And then a second. "Show me," she finally said.

His eyes held conflict, and then he opened his

mouth. Two long fangs dropped down from his gums, and his eyes turned the color of blood. So it hadn't been a trick of light back at the party.

Mina swallowed hard as she reached up and ran her fingertip over his bottom lip. A vampire. She'd read about them as legend and myth. They couldn't possibly be real, could they?

She dipped her finger into his mouth and touched his fang, pressing her finger into the razor-sharp tip until she felt a sharp prick and a bead of blood welled up. She looked on in fascination as she smeared the blood on Blue's lips.

A growl rumbled through him, and his eyes closed. Desire, shocking and sensual, coursed through her body, making her thrum with need.

Suddenly, she jerked away. "Those... those murders. The ones here in London. They said the people were all drained of blood... It was you, wasn't it?"

He hesitated and then nodded. "I only feed on those who deserve death. The first man tried to rape a woman after knocking her unconscious. The next two had robbed a store, killing the owner and his wife. The next woman was beating her child. I don't usually feed on women, but the child was so small and helpless. I thought she would honestly kill the poor thing. The next—"

She pressed her fingers to his lips and shook her head. She couldn't begrudge him. He needed to eat to live. They all did. And she herself had had moments where she wished her family would die in some terrible accident setting her free.

"You don't need to explain." She cupped his cheek. "Vlad, thank you for saving me. Again."

His eyes fixated on her, desperate and greedy. He massaged her neck and pulled her mouth toward his. She breathed him in, and butterflies nosedived through her stomach as goosebumps erected on her skin. He lingered just out of reach. She waited, wanting to feel his lips. Needing to taste his breath. Craving the press of his skin on her skin. His fingers twisted in her hair, and his lips brushed hers. All propriety fled from her as she pressed her mouth hard against his. His tongue swept into her mouth, and Mina moaned at the sensations running through her. Every molecule bent to his embrace. He gathered her to him, and Mina drained of every thought except wanting Blue.

He broke the kiss, and his lips slid down her chin toward her throat. His cool breath hit her skin. For a moment, fear washed over her, and his teeth grazed her flesh, and then his tongue hit the cut from the knife. He licked it languidly, tenderly, and Mina clutched his back as he ran his tongue the length of her throat and stopped just above the collar of her bodice.

"If you want to go any further, we should get out of the open," he said thickly. "If you aren't ready, I understand. But I'll need to stop. With you, I'm not sure if I can control myself. I want you so badly."

She shivered as words swam in her mind. "I want you, Vlad. I want you for as long as I can have you."

He leaned in and kissed her softly. "Marry me, Mina. Be my wife."

Her breath hitched. It was too fast. They'd not even known each other for two weeks, yet it was as if she'd always known him. Never before had anyone known her so intimately. Blue knew things about her that she'd not told anyone. But still...What would her father say? What would her siblings say? What would Jonathan say?

She didn't care.

"Yes," she whispered.

Blue kissed her again, and without a word, he lifted, and they rose into the air. She wrapped her arms around his neck as they moved above the buildings and flew over the city toward the hotel. Mina could hardly believe she was in the arms of a handsome, fierce man, let alone flying through the skies above London. The sensation thrilled and terrified her. High above the ground, knowing all it would take would be one shove from Blue, and she would be dashed upon the buildings below. Even so, she trusted him. Trusted him more than she had ever trusted anyone.

The night wind whipped in her face, and the dewy air made her bloodied clothes cling to her body. Fog settled around them, and she wondered how he could see where they were headed, but Blue flew on as if he'd been there a million times.

As they drew closer, they slowed and lowered to the alley between buildings. He set Mina on her feet and ran his hand up her body. Every inch of her skin begged to be touched. Shrugging out of his long coat, he wrapped it around her, hiding the worst of the staining.

Mina took his hand, and they walked out of the alley and up the hotel's steps together.

They headed straight for the elevator and took it to the third floor. Without any words, Mina pulled him down the hallway to her room and unlocked the door.

"Mina, are you sure?"

She stepped in close enough that their bodies touched. "My name is Andromina."

A slight smile spread over his face, and he backed her into her room and closed the door behind them. Her heartbeat quickened, and she walked further in, placing her purse on the small desk and removing his coat. She turned, suddenly nervous. She'd never been with a man before. She'd only just experienced her first kiss. It was like a dream she'd kept locked deep inside her and never voiced. Being kissed, flying through the air, now about to make love to a vampire, of all men.

Mina remembered Octavia's words about the

Count ruining her. She didn't mind being spoiled. Not by him. To be with Blue, she would tarnish her reputation, bend it, bruise it, break it in two, and then toss it in the sea.

Blue undid his vest and laid it over the back of the chair. He unbuttoned the top buttons of his shirt and took off his cufflinks. She held back her fear as he prowled toward her and cupped her face.

"I've wanted you from the moment I first saw you in the street. Something about you has drawn me to you like a planet orbiting the sun. I can't explain it, but in all of my lifetimes, I've never wanted someone the way I want you, Andromina."

She gave him a nervous smile. "I'm yours."

His lips pressed softly to hers. A worship of breath and skin. His fingers traveled down her back as he unbuttoned her dress and pushed it to the floor. He kissed along her throat, sliding his tongue over her shoulder and making her skin pebble. She fumbled with the buttons of his shirt, managing to get them undone, and pushed it off.

While she stood in nothing but her underclothes, Blue knelt in front of her and ran his hands under her chemise. She grabbed onto his shoulders as his cool fingers slid up her thighs and over her hips. He pushed the chemise higher, kissing his way across her stomach and over her breasts. She dug her nails into his shoulders as her buds hardened and burned.

Slowly, he inched the chemise over her head and

dropped it to the floor, revealing her breasts. She fought the urge to cover herself. Never before had she been even half-naked in front of anyone. Not since she was a young child. She wanted to ask him if she was satisfactory, wondering how many other women he'd seen and how she compared. Something inside feared the answer, so she kept it to herself.

Blue gazed at her, half-naked himself, making her body tremble with anticipation. His pale muscles stacked on top of each other, hard and strong. Dark curls covered his chest and swirled down his torso. Beneath his breeches, she could spot the outline of his excitement.

Swooping her into his arms, he carried her to the bed and lay her on it. He slid off her shoes and tugged her bloomers over her hips and legs. Nervousness skittered over her as he slipped off his remaining clothes and then slid under the sheets next to her.

He kissed her again, and when his eyes opened, they were scarlet. His fangs lowered into his mouth, and a whirl of fear whipped through her.

"Do not fear me. I would never do anything to hurt you, my love."

She swallowed back the lump in her throat. "Will you make me like you?"

He kissed her and ran his hand between her thighs to her most sensitive parts. "Not unless you want me to."

She didn't even know what that entailed. For the

moment, the answer was a resounding no. But it wasn't a permanent refusal.

She pulled his mouth to hers and kissed him fiercely. A rumble rolled through his chest as he massaged and teased her sensitive folds. A warm buzz circled her belly, and she craved more of him. He kissed down her neck and licked the last of her blood from between her breasts before moving on to suckle each of them in turn.

Mina arched closer to him, basking in the sensations rushing through her.

She reached down and grasped his firm length in her hands, stroking him.

He gasped, and his fangs grazed her shoulder. "You are so beautiful, my Andromina. So warm."

His fingers entered her, and she moaned and pressed her body against his.

"Vlad," she panted. "Make me yours."

He rolled on top of her and settled between her thighs. "It is I who am made yours."

She pulled his lips to hers as he eased inside her. The scent of blood filled the room, and she kissed him hard as he thrust into her. She swept her tongue into his mouth, pressing it to one of his fangs. Pain mingled with pleasure as she tasted the salty iron of her blood. Blue shuddered, and his tongue blended with hers. She grabbed his lip in her teeth and stared into his eyes. He watched her intently as she bit down on the flesh and tasted his blood in return. Blue pulled away quickly.

"No. Not unless you want to be like me."

"But you can bite me."

"Yes." He thrust inside her again, and she grabbed his firm rear.

"Do you want to bite me?"

His gaze intensified, and his eyes glowed like fire-light. "Always."

She turned her neck and guided his mouth to her throat.

He didn't move for several seconds, but then he licked up the side of her throat and thrust inside her again. His rhythm built, and she locked her legs with his as his fangs scraped her skin. Wordlessly, their bodies joined, and a sweet euphoria swept over her. She kissed his neck and his shoulders as she pulled him inside her harder.

His breathing became labored as his thrusts became more frantic, and the friction built between them. She guided him to her, meeting her hips with his as he finally tensed, and a sharp pain shot through her neck and down her shoulder.

Like a babe suckling, he gulped down her blood. The sensation lightened Mina's head. Blue climaxed, and his body pulled taut, almost the same tempera-ture as her own.

After several seconds, he detached his fangs from her neck and licked the wound.

He kissed his way across her chest and down to her stomach, and then over her hipbones and down the inside of her thighs. His teeth grazed her skin, making her wish he was inside her again.

"My darling little Andromina. How young and fresh you are. So sweet. So inexperienced." He crawled back up to her again, pushed the hair from her face, and kissed the tip of her nose. "Do not worry, my love." He slid his hand down her body and inside her again. "I will teach you everything you need to know about pleasure. When I told you I had extensive knowledge of anatomy, it was not a lie."

She shook her head. "Not only pleasure. I want you to teach me... everything you know—about pain as well."

A strange smile spread across his face. "My darling, it will be my pleasure. I will show you how a nip here..." He dragged his fangs down to her breast. "Combined with a stroke there..." His fingers worked inside her once more. "Can bring you to heights you've never before imagined." He circled her nipple with his fangs and then bit down ever so lightly.

She gasped, and a shockwave of pleasure shot through her. He waited. Kissing her skin.

Mina raked her fingers through his hair and pulled on his long, sable curls. "Again," she whispered.

Blue removed his fingers, and then he was inside her again. He thrust at the same time he bit down on her nipple. The sensation shot straight to her core.

His bright red eyes peered up at her as she clutched his back. He bent her legs and thrust inside her deeper, biting her with every thrust.

Soon, she could do no more than grab onto the headboard as waves of pleasure she'd never imagined possible, along with pain, rocked through her, spiraling her closer to losing control. Her body hummed with need and pulsed with the desire for release. Finally, just as his body began to tense, hers wound tight like a spring around him, and her arms turned to jelly. She cried his name as all other thoughts fled her mind, and every nerve exploded.

Their bodies joined over and over in a painful, magical rhythm until she dropped backward, spent and satisfied.

Blue lay atop her, kissing every inch of her face.

She smiled up at him. "I want you to teach me more."

He returned her smile and kissed her forehead. "We have all the time in the world, my love. And I have centuries of knowledge to show you."

"Even so, there is no time like now to begin the lessons."

"As you wish."

CHAPTER THIRTEEN

Mina and Blue spent three days in her room making love at night and sleeping during the day. They only stopped long enough for Mina to eat while Blue watched. He ordered her the best cuts of meat and spared no expense to make sure she stayed both healthy and well fed. She insisted that he only take blood from her as she wanted no more deaths, but he held back when he fed from her so as not to hurt her, and sometime soon he was going to need more. Much, much, more. But for the time being, he did whatever was required to keep her happy.

He occupied his time by showing her just how right pain could feel when mixed with pleasure. She took to it like a bee to pollen. Yet unlike others, he'd been with, she retained her innocence and wide-eyed fascination.

Within days of being with him, the others had all wanted to see a display of his abilities on someone else; even bringing them to bed for him—but not Mina. Mina only ever talked about him and them. She'd also didn't beg him to turn her as the others had. Instead, she clung to her humanity just as he'd hoped. He knew that at some point they would need to have the conversation about it, but for now, he was thrilled to have her in his life and his bed.

"I wondered what we might do this evening." He sipped his wine.

"Do we need to do something different?"

"Trust me, love, I would be more than happy to spend the night between your creamy thighs again, but I thought that you might want to do something stimulating in a different way."

"Why would I want that?" She gave him a sly smile and reached under the table, running her hand up his thigh, stopping just before she touched his growing erection.

He smiled. "Perhaps we could go to a museum. We never did finish seeing the curiosity show."

"Was there something there more curious than you?" she teased.

He chuckled. "So what then?"

"Well, I could use another dress."

He raised his glass. "Shopping it is."

. . .

"WHAT DO YOU THINK?" MINA WALKED OUT OF THE dressing room in a conventional blue day dress that hugged her in the right places but was nothing special.

She frowned. "You don't like it."

Blue rose and nodded at the attendant to leave them. He pulled Mina to him and kissed her. "The form suits you, but I prefer you in something more elegant." He scanned the row of gowns and pretty frocks, but nothing was fit for his Mina. His gaze stopped at a champagne-colored dress. Brushing past her, he lifted it off the rack and held it up.

"Blue, I couldn't possibly wear that color. It would wash me out."

He looked at the silky sheen, the hand-sewn bead-work, the delicate pearls. It was perfect. "Then why don't you wear it only once?"

"Once? Why would you waste money on something I'd only wear once?"

"Women do it every day."

"Do you think me to be one of those frivolous women?"

He kissed her on the tip of her nose. "I don't. But you will be this once. I'm buying you this one, and you shall wear it for me and only me on our wedding eve."

Mina flushed, and a smile crept across her face. "And when do you want that to be?"

He could imagine her in it. Standing before him, a veil over her face, promising to be his forever.

"Tonight. Now."

She pulled him close and leaned in, her lips almost touching his. "Then I suggest we hurry and make our purchases."

Blue beckoned the attendant back in. "We will take them all."

"I'm sorry?" asked the woman.

"Blue, it's too much."

His gaze traveled to the woman. "The dresses. We will take them all." He pressed his lips to Mina's, taking in her heavenly scent. "For you, nothing is too much. Tonight we marry. Tomorrow we head to Spain for an extended honeymoon."

BLUE BOUGHT OUT THE RESTAURANT AT THE HOTEL for the evening. He asked Mina if she minded that they have a Justice of the Peace marry them as opposed to a priest. She agreed that a Justice would do.

She stood in her room and looked at herself in the full-length mirror. She'd pulled her hair up and wore the beautiful cream gown Blue had bought. A ruby choker at her throat covered the marks where he had fed from her and matched her lips perfectly. To her surprise, the dress didn't wash her out as much as she thought it might. Instead, it enhanced the brightness of her eyes.

She pulled the floor-length veil down over her face

and stared at herself. Her father would be more than cross when he returned. The thought pained her. For all of his lies, she knew he only wished to protect them both. She prayed that upon his return he would at the very least accept her decision and give Blue a chance. She didn't wish to hurt her father, but the love the burned inside her for Blue was not something that even her father would be able to snuff out, and if they waited until his return to ask his permission, he was sure not to give it.

Mina smiled and turned her thoughts from her father to happier thoughts. She and Blue would be wed, and she would be free from her siblings' squabbling and selfishness. Free from being a servant. Free to be the person she'd always dreamed of. After tonight she would be known as Countess Draugr, wife of Count Vlad Draugr.

She made a mental note to see her father's solicitor before they left for Spain to arrange for an allowance to be sent to her brother Quincey every week until her father returned. She also needed to write her father a letter explaining her departure. He wouldn't take it well, but he deserved not to have her disappear without a word. He might actually kill her brothers in anger, thinking they had done something to her if she did not.

A soft knock sounded on her door, and she turned from the mirror.

It was time.

. . .

MINA DESCENDED THE STAIRCASE TO BE MET AT THE bottom by the hotel manager. Guilty swept through her again for not having her father there to walk her down the aisle. But if she waited for him, she was sure that she wouldn't be walking down the aisle at all.

The manager held out his arm and handed her a fragrant bouquet of brightly colored lilies wrapped in a white satin ribbon.

Blue had to have called in every favor and used most of his influence to put together what Mina beheld. In his two-hour absence, he'd managed to get the entire restaurant decorated with flowers and candles. A carpet had been rolled down the center, and Blue stood at the end of it on the stage where a singer had entertained them early that evening. Wearing an elegant deep blue waistcoat and cravat, he'd slicked his hair back, and his beard gleamed in the candlelight. His face lit up when she entered. For a moment she wondered if she was dreaming when he held his hand out toward her.

Mina smiled as she made her way down the carpet. Not a soul sat and watched her pass by. Though the idea should have made her sad, it was actually as it should have been. With no one who would approve of the union, there needn't be anyone to witness it.

She reached Blue's side, and he beamed down at her.

"I knew the dress would suit you," he whispered, leaning in and kissing her cheek.

"Your jacket matches your eyes."

They stared at each other for a long moment and then turned to the officiator.

He nodded to Blue. "It is an honor to be officiating for you this beautiful evening. I welcome you, Count Vladimir Drakul Draugr, and you, Lady Andromina..."

"Calliope Rose Murray."

"Andromina Calliope Rose Murray, to this momentous declaration of love and commitment. Marriage between a man and a woman is—"

"I'm sorry," Mina interrupted. "But, I am not one for long ceremonies. Might we skip the introduction?"

Blue chuckled and squeezed her hands. "And that, my darling, is just one of the reasons I adore you."

The Justice nodded. "Of course."

Blue kissed the back of Mina's hand. "My dearest Andromina. I've spent lifetimes waiting for my bride to find me. And I now know that it was worth the wait. Anything you desire, I will give. Anything you dream, I will make come true. Anything that dares harm you, I will remove from this world. I am yours, my love, today, tomorrow, and forever."

Mina's heart felt full to bursting. She couldn't imagine anything that would make her happier in that moment. Blue would be true to his word for as long as they were together.

"Vladimir. My life was not but a dreary wasteland until you came into it. Before you, I was left wanting. No dreams lay within reach. Every desire remained fulfilled. But you have opened my eyes to a world I never knew existed. You are my love, my life, my everything. I give myself to you, my love, body, spirit, and soul. From now until forever."

"Do you have the rings?"

Blue removed a box from his pocket and opened it. Inside sat a giant emerald ring surrounded by diamonds.

"I thought you might enjoy something that matches your eyes."

Tears threatened to spill. "I don't have one for you."

He shook his head. "We will pick one out tomorrow." Blue plucked the ring from its cushy bed and slid it on her finger. "With this ring, I vow to be yours alone until the sun takes me or time devours me."

Mina removed her mother's bracelet from around her wrist and stepped into Blue. "With this gift, I vow to be yours forever until the sun takes me or time devours me."

She dropped the bracelet into his palm. It seemed befitting that she gave it to him when her real mother might very well have been the only one who would have been happy for her at that moment, were she alive.

"With these tokens of love, I now pronounce you husband and wife. You may kiss the bride."

Mina trembled as Blue lifted her veil and pulled her firmly against him. A now familiar flush of heat traversed her skin. He brought his lips close to hers and breathed in deep.

"You better kiss me, Blue, or I'm bound to do something completely unladylike."

He chuckled and brushed his knuckles across her cheek. "You save all that unladylike behavior for me alone, Countess Draugr."

Mina smiled. He pressed his lips to hers.

They parted, and clapping ensued behind them. A crowd of people had gathered at the restaurant entrance and in the lobby.

"I wish you both the best in your future together," said the officiator.

Mina smiled. They were going to need it.

Blue took her arm. "Shall we head to our honeymoon suite?"

"Only if you promise we won't leave it until right before our train departs tomorrow for Spain."

"That's my plan."

Mina laid her hand on his arm, and they headed for the exit. As they approached, the hotel manager stepped forward, a concerned look on his face.

"Count, Countess, I apologize for interrupting

your nuptials, but this telegram has just arrived for you."

Blue took the piece of paper and read it.

"What is it?" Mina asked. Blue looked at her, his face a mask of anger and fear. "What's happened?"

"I must return home, darling. I promise I won't be but the night."

"Blue?"

He kissed her cheek. "I'll come back before dawn, and we will get on the train to Spain, and I promise I will spend every waking night making this up to you."

"But Blue—"

"I'm sorry, my love. I must leave." He turned and took a step.

"Vlad!"

He stopped in his tracks, and the others who'd gathered around began to disperse. He heaved a sigh and returned to her side.

"Don't lie," she said. "Don't keep things from me."

He kissed her hard, and his tongue swept into her mouth, making her weak. Then he broke the kiss and rested his forehead against hers. "I promise you, my love. I will tell you everything when I return."

He turned without another word and fled from the hotel. Mina opened her mouth to call to him, but she didn't.

The manager approached her with a sad smile. "I have the honeymoon suite as requested if you would like someone to escort you there."

Mina stared at the exit, her mind reeling. She was his wife. There should be no secrets between them, not now.

"Countess?"

Blue would fly home, of that she was sure. He'd be there much sooner than she could ever hope to. But it didn't matter. If he wanted her in his life forever the way he claimed he did, then he had to share it all with her: the great, the scary, and the secrets.

Mina turned to the manager. "That won't be necessary. Please call a coachman. I need to get to the train station."

The manager opened his mouth. Then, as if thinking better of it, he smiled and inclined his head.

"Of course, Countess."

CHAPTER FOURTEEN

Blue landed atop his manor house and looked downward. He sniffed the air, catching the scent he knew he would find, as well as the smell of the impending storm.

Jumping from the roof, he landed by the front door and pushed it open as the first droplets of rain hit his shoulder.

Silence permeated the house. He stalked to his study, where the door stood open, and took in the scene. A deep-colored stain pooled on the rug in the middle of the floor. Blood splattered his desk, books, and even the wall. The scene could only be attributed to one person.

Anger pulsed through his body as he turned and headed up the stairs. He rushed down the hall and up another set of stairs to the third floor. The long, oppressive corridor squeezed upon Blue from every side as he strode to the first room and knocked. A chair scraped against the floor, and then the door opened. Iona, the maid that had come with him from Romania, peeked out and then opened the door.

Renfield lay ashen on his bed, the blankets tucked in up to his neck. Blue crossed to him and pulled back the sheet to reveal his chest, bound tightly with blood-soaked gauze.

"Did she feed on him?" he asked in their native tongue.

"Not that I can see," replied Iona.

"Has he awoken?"

Iona shook her head. *"I'm sorry, master, but the young estate man, Mr. Harker, panicked after she used him to open the fireplace. He witnessed her attack Renfield and then fled the house in terror. Marris followed soon after. With Renfield down, there was nothing I could do."*

"It's not your fault," said Blue. "It's mine."

Blue covered Renfield again with the sheet, fighting against the rage that burned inside him. He rolled up his sleeve and bit into his wrist. Grabbing a cup from the nightstand, he squeezed his blood into it.

Lightning struck outside, and Blue looked up just as the first of the raindrops hit the window.

"Make him drink that." He strode for the door. "Keep him warm and comfortable."

"What are you going to do?"

Blue leveled his gaze on Iona. "What I should have done years ago."

Blue flew to the staircase. He jumped down to the lower level and raced for the landing. Bounding straight to the bottom floor, he made for the front door. Throwing it wide, he sniffed the stormy wind. He barely caught Marris' scent heading toward the wood but worse than that was the rich, warm scent of blood.

He stepped out into the night. Thunder clattered around him, and lightning lit up the entire estate. A howl sounded in the distance. Blue raised his arms to the sky, allowing the rain to pelt his face.

"Creatures of the night, hear me and obey," he chanted.

Far and wide wolves howled in the woods, ravens screeched in the night, and bats chirped at his call.

"Find the one who has broken her oath. Find her and bring her to me."

Blue's gaze turned toward the wood. He lifted into the sky and raced toward the treetops.

MINA STEPPED THROUGH THE OPEN DOOR AND LOOKED around the house. "Hello?"

Silence met her, and a terrible chill swept over her body. She proceeded into the house, listening for any signs of the servants or Blue, but none arrived.

She shook off her cloak and set it with her purse on the hall table. Wrapping her arms around herself, she shivered at the turbulent air.

"Blue? Renfield? Jonathan?"

Again, no answer came. She walked down the back hallway of the house to the kitchen, but the stove fire had died, and no one was there. Her heels clicked on the floor as she headed to the front door and then around the left side of the house. She paused at the sight of Blue's open study door. A feeling of dread overtook her, and the need to run away became almost palpable. But something about the open door called to her like a siren's song, beckoning her forward.

Blue had told her never to enter the room, yet she couldn't keep her feet from moving toward it. She just wanted to look, to see if he was inside. She wouldn't go in, only look.

She drew closer, and the first splash of red caught her eye. It looked as though someone had scattered paint across Blue's desk. She fought against the panic that scratched up her throat. She moved closer to the doorway, and her gaze lit on the giant pool of blood on the oriental rug and the scent of death that lingered.

Mina swallowed hard. "Blue? Blue? Vlad!"

He didn't answer.

Mina jumped as lighting and thunder crashed outside, rattling the windows. She raced for the front door and yelled Blue's name, but it was lost in the thunder that had taken up residence directly over the estate. The rain pelted the windows like small pebbles and drenched the green between Blue's estate and her father's. She worried for a moment that perhaps Blue hadn't come home. Maybe he'd gone to her father's house instead. Was it possible news had come about her family, and he'd gone there to deal with it? To deal with them?

Mina went to gather her cloak to see if he was next door, but when a sound caught her attention, she stopped.

"Hello?"

Help us, came a whispered response from deep within the home. *Please, Mina. Free us.*

Her body shook at the helpless sound of the pleas. Just like the one from the night of the ball. The voice that had called to her from inside the fireplace.

Seconds ticked by, and she wondered if her mind wasn't playing tricks on her again, but finally, she lifted her foot and willed herself to walk into the study.

She stopped in the doorway and stared into the room. The fireplace called to her, whispering her name and making her want to go inside.

She lifted her foot to enter, but as if a giant hand grabbed her, a barrier of some sort prevented her from entering. Every muscle of her body fought against her will, refusing to move forward. She pushed against the strange, unsettling feeling, but the invisible hand squeezed harder around her. Her mind told her to turn around, walk away, that she didn't want to go into Blue's study- but at the same time, she knew she did.

Her body shook with strain as she fought against the compelling magic that tried to force her away from the door. Inch by inch, she ordered her foot forward through sheer will. It lowered a fraction and then more and more until finally, after what seemed like an hour, her foot hit the rug inside the room. Like a rubber band breaking, the invisible hand upon her snapped, and she fell forward, landing face first on the floor. She lay for a moment catching her breath, and then she rose slowly just inside the door. She waited a moment, but her invisible assailant seemed to have disappeared.

Thunder rumbled outside, and rain bombarded the glass in giant sheets. Lightning cracked as if applauding her tremendous effort and illuminated the room. She laughed out loud at the absurdity of it all.

Mina. Help us.

She turned her gaze to the fireplace. The words floated around the room, bouncing off the walls, and settling in her mind. She moved forward, stumbling through the bloodstained carpet, her shoes sticking to the threads.

Mmmmmiiiiiiinnnnnaaaaaa...

She stopped at the stone and wooden hearth and shook her head. "I... I can't," she said to no one. "I don't know how to get to you."

Push the flower.

Mina examined the mantle. The ornate wood-work scrolled all around and up the wall. On either end of the mantel were two ornate camellias adorned with several smaller bunches of roses. She walked to the one on the left and ran her fingers over it. She laid both hands on top of a bloom bigger than her palms and pushed. To her surprise, the flower sunk in, and the mantle swung outward.

She jumped back and stared at the now open passage. She waited, expecting someone to step out and thank her, but no one appeared. Curious, she grabbed the edge of the mantel and pulled it toward her. The dense wood and stone creaked open wider as she leaned back. When she'd created a gap that was several feet wide, she grabbed a candelabra from a nearby table and squeezed through the opening.

The light of the candles rolled into the darkness, casting long shadows and lending an eerie glow to the entire small room. The smell of decay and garbage made her wrinkle her nose. She took a step further into the room and kicked something. Dozens of rat corpses scattered the floor. Mina backed up and hit the wall with a clatter.

Across the room, something moved in the shadows.

"Hello?"

"Mina," someone whispered from the corner. "Mina, help us."

Mina lifted the candelabra higher to peer into the

room's recesses. The sound of scraping metal emanated from the corner.

"Who are you," Mina asked. "What are you doing in here?"

"We are the wives," a female whispered.

"Trapped in here for sins of the past," said another.

A chill swept over Mina. "Who... whose wives?" She could barely ask the question, though she already knew the answer.

"Count Draugr."

A skeletal-looking woman in a long, dirty nightgown stepped into the light. "I am Ylza, the first wife. Back before he became what he is now. Before he grew bored of me." She motioned over her shoulder. "Second was Irina. Then Suzetta, but she's dead. He took Marris fourth, and now, it appears, he has taken you."

Mina's chest squeezed. Four wives before her. Blue had four other wives? She tried to wrap her mind around the idea. Five wives. Blue had five wives. Was she even his wife if he was already married? Had everything he'd said he felt for her been a sham?

"Help us," begged Ylza. "Free us, and we'll go away. You'll never hear from us again. I promise."

"Please." A second emaciated woman stepped forward. "We are just so hungry. All we want is to get somewhere safe and warm and feed."

The woman lurched forward. Mina stumbled and

grabbed the wall for support. Her palm caught on a sharp rock, and she felt the sting as it bit into her skin.

The second woman pulled against her shackles and purred. "Do you smell that?"

"She's human," said Ylza.

"He didn't turn her."

"Why?" Ylza demanded. "Why didn't he turn you? Why didn't he make you a monster like us?"

The women howled in rage and fought against their restraints, trying to get at Mina. Firm arms wrapped around Mina's waist, yanking her out of the room.

"Back! Back foul demons!" a man yelled.

He splashed something on the women, and they began to scream as their skin seared and melted away. Mina couldn't believe her eyes as the women's skin turned black, and they scurried into the shadows of the room once more.

Mina pushed away from the person who grabbed her to find Jonathan standing with Arthur and Quincey.

"Where is he?" demanded Arthur. "Where is the devil?"

Mina stared at the three in confusion. What were they doing there? Quincey tossed the now empty bottle into the fireplace.

"Your hand," said Jonathan. "You're bleeding." He set the gun she didn't realize he'd been holding on the table and pulled a handkerchief from his pocket, pressing it to her palm.

Mina turned as the women cursed and screeched behind the fireplace.

"Let us out!"

"Who is that?" Quincey asked. "Who is back there?"

"It's his other wives," replied Jonathan. "I told you. He's been keeping them in there. Monsters that feed on blood."

"What about you?" Arthur demanded, stepping closer to her. "Are you one of them? Has he turned you into the devil's concubine?"

Mina jerked her hand away from Jonathan. "He hasn't done anything to me. You fools don't even know what you're talking about."

"You are coming home with us," said Arthur. "And in the morning, we two are going to London, where you will withdraw all the money Father left us and give it to me."

Mina pushed back her shoulders. "I'm not going anywhere with you. You should leave. Now."

Arthur lunged for her, but Jonathan stepped in the way. "Leave her alone."

"Or what?" Arthur demanded. "What will you do?"

Jonathan grabbed the gun from the table. "Back away from Mina."

Arthur snorted. "You don't have the guts, houseboy."

Jonathan cocked the hammer. "Are you so sure?"

Arthur stared at them for a moment and then backed up a pace. "None of this would have happened, Mina, if you'd just done what you were told. Taken care of the house. Taken care of us. Waited for Father to come home."

"Maybe I was tired of playing mother to you and Quincey and Lucy. Did you ever stop to think that maybe I might want something for myself?"

"So you what? Whored yourself out to a monster?"

"Better the whore of a monster than the sister of a two-bit layabout who wouldn't know a day's work if it bit him in the ass."

Arthur's fists clenched. "You bitch."

Mina's rage threatened to spill over. She kept her voice low and calm, barely above a whisper. "Maybe I am, and maybe I'm not, but that is the last time you will ever get to call me one. Get out of my house, and don't you ever set foot on my lands again."

Arthur snorted. "You don't own these lands or this house."

Mina lifted her hand. "As of four hours ago, I do."

Jonathan turned on her, wide-eyed. "Mina... You didn't."

The hurt in his eyes punched her in the gut. It

wasn't how she'd wanted to tell Jonathan. She'd hoped to be able to explain to him about how wrong he'd been about Blue. To explain that Blue had shown her things and given her things that she would never have believed she could have with another person. That he understood her in a way no one else ever would.

Distracted by staring at Mina, Jonathan never saw the blow coming. Mina's scream came too late as Arthur grabbed Jonathan by the arm and twisted the gun away. He shoved Jonathan to the floor, and Mina stood over Jonathan, protecting him.

"Get out of here, Arthur," she commanded. "This is your last warning. You won't like the outcome if you and Quincey don't leave immediately."

Arthur backhanded her, and her head rocked to the side. "And you, little sister, won't like the outcome if you don't shut your mouth."

Mina slowly turned her gaze back to her brother and smiled. She touched her lip as pain shot through her face.

Fear crept across Arthur's brow.

"Maybe we should go." Quincey pulled on Arthur's sleeve.

Mina's gaze narrowed on her brother, and she wiped at the blood that trickled down her chin. "You shouldn't have done that."

"No. He shouldn't have."

The group turned toward Blue, standing in the doorway, dripping blood-tinged rainwater on the carpet. A red liquid stained his face and hands. It seeped into his blue waistcoat, turning it purple on the edges. Bits of what looked like flesh and gore flecked his white shirt, tinting it a deep maroon. His crimson eyes heated with rage.

On either side of him stood two imposing wolves: one black as night, the other bright white, both with bloody muzzles. Teeth bared Mina knew they were ready to do Blue's bidding.

A moment passed in tense silence, and then Blue spoke in a language she didn't recognize.

"Children, kill."

The wolves raced at Quincey.

Mina didn't even see him move, yet in the blink of an eye, Blue rushed Arthur and sunk his fangs deep into his throat. Arthur's mouth opened in a silent scream, and blood bubbled over his lips. He stared at her pleadingly, but she could do nothing more than stare back with a deep sense of satisfaction. She refused to look away as the life drained out of his eyes, trying to remember any good moments they'd share. Any memories of affection. Any time where he'd played with her, or read to her, or... anything. But there weren't any.

The gun fell from his hand and hit the floor with a clatter as his body slackened and then went lifeless.

Quincey lay on the floor, blood pouring from his throat as the wolves stood over him like sentinels. A pang of sadness struck her over Quincey. He'd been lazy and a follower of Arthur's but not as bad as Arthur. Without the influence of his elder brother, possibly in time, he could have turned into a good man. Possibly. But that was gone now. Both of them were gone.

Blue dropped Arthur to the floor and rushed to Mina's side. He scoured her face. "I told you to stay put."

"You need me."

The pad of his thumb brushed her lower lip, where blood trickled from a cut. He kissed her hair. "What would I have done if something had happened to you? My life would have been over. You should have stayed put."

"And you should have told me the truth."

He released her, his eyes full of regret. "I wanted to tell you. I did. But... I was so afraid of losing you. That it would have been too much to take."

"You wouldn't have lost me. Nothing you could ever do would change the way I love you."

"How can you say that?" Jonathan stood behind Blue, the gun raised.

"Jonathan don't—"

"He killed them. Arthur and Quincey. Your own brothers. They may have been horrible human beings, but they were still human. He's a monster, Mina."

Blue pressed Mina behind him. "Jonathan. I know this must seem confusing."

The wolves growled at Jonathan, and he swung the gun between them and Blue.

"Easy. Easy." Blue looked at the wolves. *"Stay back."*

The wolves retreated a pace but continued to hold their alert stance.

Blue looked to Jonathan again. "You saw Arthur attack Mina. It isn't the first time. He would have hurt her, possibly killed her this time. And Quincey would have died defending his brother. I did what I must to protect Mina. I'm a vampire, not a monster."

Jonathan's hand shook as he held out the gun. The wolves' ears flattened against their heads as they took a step toward him.

"No," Mina called. "Vlad, don't hurt him. Please."

Blue's gaze stayed glued on Jonathan. "Jonathan, look at me. Look into my eyes. You don't want to do this. You are a good man. You don't want to become a killer."

"Killing you would set Mina free. It would be a kindness that I do."

Mina stepped forward. "Jonathan, please don't."

His gaze turned to her. "How can you not see what he is, Mina? How can you be so under his spell?"

"I'm not under his spell. I love him. Killing him won't change that. You are my friend. My best friend. I wanted to tell you, but there wasn't time. Please. You want me to be happy, don't you?"

Jonathan shook his head. "It's a spell. I've seen it. If I kill him. I set you free."

"Jonathan—"

Time slowed as the shot rang out. Blue was on Jonathan in an instant. Another shot fired, and then another. Mina screamed as Blue wrenched the gun away from Jonathan and tackled him to the floor.

"No, Blue, leave him. Please." Mina's chest burned as she fought to breathe. Her heart pounded, and her head lightened. She staggered and caught herself on Blue's desk.

Blue turned to her, fangs elongated, wild anger scorching his red gaze. She coughed, and blood spattered the front of her clothes. Blue's eyes went wide, and he rushed to her. Her legs buckled, and she collapsed.

"Mina. My love."

Hot liquid bubbled up her throat as the burning spread through her chest, but her limbs turned to ice.

She tried to lift her arms, but they were too heavy. Blue stripped off his coat and pressed it to her chest.

"No. Mina. Don't leave. I just found you."

Mina coughed and choked as a metallic taste filled her mouth. She tried to say his name, but nothing came out.

"Mina. Tell me what to do. Mina, stay with me. Stay..."

Her vision grew fuzzy, and she looked over to Jonathan.

Tears dripped from his eyes. "I'm sorry, Mina. I'm so sorry." Without another word, he fled.

"Mina... I love you," Blue cried.

Bloody tears dripped down Blue's cheeks. The edges of her vision dimmed, and she fought to stay conscious.

She wanted to tell him she loved him. To tell him she was frightened. To tell him she forgave him for not telling her about the other women.

Instead, she held on as long as she could, and then everything faded to nothingness.

CHAPTER FIFTEEN

Draugr

Blue perched on the edge of his bed, his head in his hands. Behind him, Mina had been bathed and put into her nightgown. Her hair fanned out behind her, making her skin appear that much more ashen.

"Will there be anything else, my Lord?" Iona asked.

"Wait with me."

Iona nodded and sat in a plush armchair. Blue stared up at the clock. It was almost five in the morning. He'd spent an hour just holding Mina and crying over her, only to then bring her upstairs, bathe her, and put her in bed. He had yet to deal with Ylza and Irina, but deal with them, he would. Just as he had with Suzetta and with Marris. Luckily, his children had caught Marris before she'd made it to town.

If he'd dealt with his mistakes when he should

have, this never would have happened. But he'd hoped for decades that, eventually, they would see the error of their ways. That killing innocent people was wrong. That they would change so he could let them out to enjoy the world. But they hadn't. If anything, they'd gotten worse.

If only he'd waited for Mina to come along. Swallowed down his loneliness and refused to give in to temptation. They wouldn't be where they were.

A sliver of light inched across his bedroom floor from between the curtains. Blue looked over at Mina, so peaceful and serene. He moved next to her and lay at her side. He ran his finger down her cold cheek. How was it possible that he could fall in love with someone so fast? To feel her warm body and taste her skin and know without a doubt that he was meant to be hers, only to then be met with her stiff, lifeless body.

Arrangements would have to now be made. Secret burials and traveling once again to a new place. Starting over. Beginning again. It was almost too much to bear.

As the sunlight crept closer to the bedpost, Blue stared at Mina, his heart broken for what was to come. Minutes ticked by, and the sunlight edged closer... closer... closer until finally, it landed on Mina's face, illuminating it. Her skin reddened and blistered.

Blue bit the inside of his cheek, watching her

beautiful face char and her hair burn away and turn to ash. Her sleeve began to smoke, and she bolted upright and screamed.

He gathered her in his arms, shielding her from the rays as the bitter smell of burnt hair filled his nose. His arm blistered as he protected her. He let the pain wash over him. It was the least he could endure, considering what he'd put her through.

Iona ran to the curtains and shut them tight as Mina shook, her body wracked with immeasurable pain. It didn't matter how many times over the hundreds of years he'd been burned by the sun; the pain never decreased with time.

She pulled her head from his chest, and he could barely take the sight of her charred face and the bald spot with the oozing, blistered scalp.

"What's happened? Where am I?"

Blue touched her cheek. "I'm sorry, my love. I couldn't let you go."

Mina touched her face. "My face."

"It's all right. It's part of the process. All you need do is feed, and it will heal."

Iona walked to Blue's side. Mina looked from him to the servant, who rolled up her sleeve, revealing a lifetime of scarring from where she'd fed Blue when he was in dire need.

Mina's eyes widened, and she backed up a bit. "You... made me like you."

234

"It was the only way. I am sorry, but I am a selfish creature who could not bear to let you leave me."

She looked between them. "You have other wives. I saw them. When you were done with them, you locked them away. Is that what will happen to me? Will you tire of me and lock me away when you find someone who satisfies you more?"

"No. No," he assured her. "I made mistakes in the past in whom I chose. I waited so long for you, and I became so lonely. I succumbed to temptation. I let beauty sway me and ignored the warning signs so plain to see in their selfish and indulgent personalities. I took wives hoping to fill the void, but only you could fill it. I see that now. It's always been you I've yearned for. Searched for. Lived lifetimes for. Mina, you aren't like them. I knew that from the first night, we spent together. They broke the rules. Fed and killed. Innocent people. Children. I couldn't allow that. So, I did what I thought was best. I shut them away, hoping they would change in time like me."

Mina's calculating gaze landed on him. "If I am to be your wife, I must be your only wife."

"Of course. I'll send Ylza and Irina away—"

"No. If they are as you say, then there must be no more sending away. No more locking up. You must end it. It is the only way for us to move forward."

He had been wavering about ending it that night anyway, but hearing her say it somehow made his mind up for him.

"How?"

"A fire. The whole place must be burnt to the ground. My brother's bodies as well. It is the only way to cover the evidence should Jonathan go to the police. Which he will eventually. His conscience will dictate that he go and tell the authorities what he has done here and what you did."

"Of course. I would give everything I own if only you would still be mine."

Mina's expression was one of confidence, something he'd never seen on her before. She scooted to the edge of the bed and pulled Iona's wrist to her mouth. Her fangs descending was the most erotic thing Blue had ever witnessed. She struck Iona's wrist as quick as a viper but not as hard. Drinking greedily, her skin healed over, and her long ebony hair flowed out of her scalp once more. Without being told, she let go of Iona's arm and turned to Blue. He wiped the blood from her mouth as Iona exited.

"I knew you were different," he whispered. "I knew you were the one. My bride."

He leaned in and kissed Mina's soft lips, her temperature now the same as his.

"Andromina," he whispered.

She ripped open his shirt and swirled her tongue over his chest. "Yes, Vladimir?"

Need mounted inside him, and he wanted nothing more than to bury himself deep inside her. To feel her and make sure she was indeed still with him. That she'd chosen him. That she was his.

"I want to make love to you."

She pushed him back on the bed and crawled onto his lap; pushing his shirt from his shoulders, her fangs grazed his skin as she kissed up his neck.

"Yes, my love," she whispered. "But first. I am still hungry."

Without a word, her fangs pierced his neck. Blue grabbed onto her hips as she drew from him, making his body respond to the point of almost exploding. He dug his fingers into her skin and reveled in the feel of her mouth on him. When she'd had her fill, she kissed him hard and undid his breeches. She slid her body down on his, wrapping him inside her silken folds.

"Tell me you're mine." She rocked her hips against his.

Waves of pleasure crashed over his body. "I'm yours."

She slid down on him again, her body gripping him tight. "Tell me there will never be another."

He clung to the sheets, trying to hold back. "Not even after the sun takes me or time devours me." A burning built in the back of his thighs as everything inside him wound tight, awaiting his release. But not yet. Not until she willed it so.

"Tell me you love me."

Blue pulled her mouth to his.

"I love you," he moaned. "My Mina. My Countess. My love."

She bit his lip. "Now." He climaxed as she bid him to, as blood mingled in their mouths.

Waves of release crashed down on him, only leaving room for one single thought.

Their pleasure was just beginning.

EPILOGUE

Mina lay in the darkened passenger cabin of the train wrapped in Blue's embrace. She replayed the newspaper clipping she'd read right before boarding the train at London station.

Count Draugr of Romania's estate burned to the ground. Bodies found inside. The Count presumed dead along with houseguest Miss Andromina Murray and her two brothers Arthur and Quincey Murray, three of Admiral Murray's four children, who had come by for a visit, as well as several servants. Autopsies are yet to be performed...

They'd lit the house on fire that night and headed to London with Iona, Renfield, and two coaches of valuables Blue wanted to keep. He'd sent the crates ahead of them to Romania. The four of them had waited in a small flat until Renfield was fit to travel.

Blue had taken Mina out at night and shown her

how to feed without killing. How to choose who to feed on. He'd even begun her lessons in compulsion. The speed and skill at which she took to the tasks astounded even him.

After a week they had packed Renfield and Iona on a train bound for Romania, and she and Blue had gotten on a train headed for Spain. Renfield had protested, but they had promised him they would stay in touch and call for him when he'd fully recovered.

According to Blue, he owned land in almost every country on the continent. They could go where they wanted. See what they wanted and stay as long as they wanted.

Mina listened to the sounds of the train as it rushed down the tracks, further away from London. Her father would be home in under two weeks to find three of his four children dead. It pained her to think about the torment he would suffer, but she also knew that their absence would do his financial situation very well. Her thoughts turned to Lucy and what she must be going through.

The night after the fire she'd crept to Lucy's bedroom window to see her. Through the curtains, she'd spotted Lucy sitting on the edge of her bed, staring off. She'd sat there for close to thirty minutes before finally getting to her feet and going into Mina's room. Mina looked on as Lucy ran her fingers over Mina's various items and then suddenly began to smash everything to pieces while screaming that it was Mina's fault.

Blue had found her there, clinging to the side of the house, watching Lucy, tears streaming. He'd picked her up and flown her back to London.

And now on the train to Spain, she wondered if her father would blame her as well. She'd not gotten a chance to leave a letter for the solicitor, but she assumed Lucy would be quick to get to him and make sure he knew of Mina's death so that she could get the money released into her custody.

"You should sleep, my love. I don't want you to grow weak," said Blue.

She pulled his head to her breast and stroked his hair. "I will."

His arms encircled her and she smiled. For the first time, she had something that was indeed hers. A man to share all of eternity with. To share adventure, passion, and blood. A husband of her own. A husband she would never let go.

THE END

FRANKENSTEIN'S BRIDE

CHAPTER ONE

P ain.

Blood boiling like acid.

Nerve endings searing like a brush fire.

A lightning rod attached to his spine.

One moment there had been nothing, and the next, blinding light stabbing his retinas. A scream filling his lungs with air, pushing the sound out of his vocal cords raw and craggy like a wounded animal being ripped apart. The scent of wet stone, metal and ozone filled his nostrils and the sound of crashing thunder imbedded in his ears. But more than the pain —fear.

What was happening to him? Where was he? *Who* was he? A jumble of memories tumbled into his mind. Flashing images he couldn't catch. *Running. Falling. Screaming.*

The pain dimmed like a light slowing burning out.

Aftershocks spasmed his body. Muscles twitched of their own accord. His head whipped back and forth, unable to stop. Something cold pressed against his chest and he fought to open his eyes. Gluey mucus obscured his view, but a face swam into focus.

Male. Stained, dingy long white coat. A doctor maybe? Facial hair. Dark eyes, serious eyes, tired eyes.

The taste of iron filled his mouth. He sucked in a ragged breath and the pounding in his skull lessened minutely.

"It's alive," the doctor man whispered. "I can't believe it. I did it."

A light flashed close to him from a flickering lantern. He tried to pull away, but large leather straps kept him bound. He scanned the room in an effort to pull a memory of where he was.

"Day one hundred and twenty six," the doctor spoke into a machine. "The body configuration seems to have worked this time. The balance and proportions are adequate."

The doctor, tall with long limbs, poked him with a needle and he pulled away. The doctor walked around him prodding and pricking different parts of his body, making him twitch and his heart thunder as panic swept through him.

"All major muscle groups seem to respond to stimulus. Whether there is any major motor functions or not is yet to be seen. If not, then next time I suggest finding a body that had not sustained such damage.

An eye needed replacing, as did both limbs and the right foot. Matching was an issue, but all nerves seem to be working as they should."

The doctor ran his fingers through his hair and scribbled furiously in a leather bound notebook as he spoke into the machine. 'The Parts.' 'The Body.'

He wasn't a body, he was a person... even though he couldn't remember who he was or how he'd gotten there.

The man prattled on. He looked around the icy cavernous laboratory. Dense wooden benches and tables lined the room. In one corner a hulking machine swirled with viscous green fluid. A coil, thick as a child's arm, spun with electricity and emptied into a metallic canister. Glass bottles, dead specimens, severed body parts and intricate drawings covered the shelves and stonewalls.

"Where—" He coughed. "Where... am... I?" His voice came out barely above a whisper but his breath hung in the air.

The man continued to talk into the machine paying him no mind.

He pulled on his restraints that smelled faintly of lineament. The thick bands flexed but held fast against his chest, wrists and ankles. A rush of alarm raced up his spine, covering his body in a slick sheen of sweat.

Images flashed into his mind. *A little girl lying dead*

in his arms. People yelling and spitting on him. Him begging for someone to believe him that he hadn't done it.

He needed to get out of there.

Straining against the leather again, the bands groaned against his strength.

He screamed as he pulled against the barriers, and the doctor turned and looked at him.

"Stop!" The man pushed him in the chest, forcing him back onto the wooden slab.

More images. *Being strapped to a table by police. Thick wooden sticks hitting his arms, legs and stomach. "CONFESS!"*

He cried out again and yanked harder, every muscle flexing and burning. He needed to get up. He needed to get out. He heaved again and the buckle on his left wrist snapped. Pressing on the table with his palm he leveraged himself against the wood and sat up, bursting the leather that bound his chest. He yanked his right hand free and the doctor backed up, terror staining his eyes.

"Where... am... I?" he asked again.

The doctor stumbled into a table, knocking over the machine he's spoken into and tipping over several beakers. The items crashed to the floor, and suddenly, the man spun around and rummaged for something on the workbench.

Breaking the cuffs from his feet, he slid off the table. His legs wobbled underneath him like he weighed more than he should. He looked down at his naked body to find his right foot a shade darker than his left. He held his hands in front of him, not recognizing them. They were bigger than he remembered. The arms, stronger and more muscular. A scar on his hip caught his attention. That one was right. But the giant Y-shaped scar that intersected his chest and coursed down his abdomen was definitely new. He grabbed onto the table for support and sucked in a jagged breath. Someone had cut him open... A mortician's scar.

"Wwwww... What... did... you... do... to... meeeee?" He turned just as the man plunged a syringe into his arm.

Roaring he yanked the syringe from his arm, backhanded the doctor and sent him tumbling to the floor. He scoured the room for an exit and located stairs on the opposite side of the laboratory. He lumbered toward them, grabbing onto various tables and shelves for support. His head grew fuzzy and his weight began to sink into the floor. He hauled himself up the stairs.

"No!" the doctor shouted.

But he didn't stop. He kept going. Even as cloudiness tinged the edges of his vision and his body slowed. His mouth dried but the taste of iron lingered on his tongue. His legs weighed down like bricks had been set on them and his eyelids threatened to close.

He couldn't fall asleep again. He couldn't. To fall asleep was to die.

He pressed against a heavy wooden door and fell into a once grand entrance hall. A broad dark staircase wound up and around the entire structure. Above him, lightning boomed and lit up the entire house through a domed skylight.

He spun in a circle, in an effort to recognize the house, but none of the gothic architecture rung familiar. He staggered, spotted the front door, and shambled toward it. With no thought as to what lay beyond, he focused on the elaborate brass door handle and dragged his body onward. It was his only chance.

"Amore? What is all the noise?"

He stopped at the sound of a gentle voice and turned to the staircase. A beautiful tan woman with flowing dark hair walked down the steps in a white nightgown.

Her eyes widened at the sight of him and she clutched her gown. He wanted to reassure her. To apologize for scaring her. To hide his nakedness and tell her he wouldn't hurt her- but his strength gave way and instead he dropped to his knees. He toppled backward and she rushed down the steps and caught his head before it smacked the biting mosaic floor.

The doctor burst from the basement, his gaze wild. "Elisabeth, don't touch it!"

As darkness flooded his vision and his eyelids drooped, she looked down at him with such pity it made him want to apologize again.

"Elisabeth, get away."

Sleep clouded his mind like a snug warm blanket.

Her gaze hardened on the man who strode across the hallway. "Victor Frankenstein. What the hell did you do to this man?" Her voice lilted with a beautiful accent he couldn't place. Not Spanish or French... something else.

She looked down at him again and stroked the hair from his face. Her brown eyes disappeared from view.

"Help... me..." he whispered.

FRANKENSTEIN'S BRIDE
(Immortal Monsters Book Two)
COMING 2025

Dear Reader,

Thank you for taking the time to read *Dracula's Bride*. I loved writing this book. It's been a long time since I've been able to delve into the darkness of a vampire who loves being himself and a woman who helps him embrace it. That's just one of the reasons I love Blue and Mina so much.

If you enjoyed the book, please take a moment to leave a review on your favorite retailer. Your reviews make all the difference to an author and the success of books.

Feel free to take a moment and email me and let me know what you liked about the book or who your favorite character was and why. I love hearing from readers. It makes writing so much more fun when I hear from my readers.

VampWereZombie@Gmail.com

To find out more about me and my Upcoming Releases, Please Join my Street Team for Swag and Freebies.

I also love connecting with readers! Stalk me everywhere!

I look forward to hearing from you!

Rebekah R. Ganiere - BOOKS WITH A BITE

The Society Series

Reign of the Vampires

Rise of the Fae

Vengeance of the Demons

The Otherworlder Series

Kidnapped at Christmas

Vigilante at Valentine

Massacre at Mardi Gras

Hoodwinked at Halloween

Nightmare at New Years (Coming 2023)

Speed Dating with the Denizens of the Underworld

Thor

Loki

Fenrir

Tyr (2024)

Odin (2024)

Dead Awakenings

Kissed by the Reaper

Dracula's Bride

Rekindling Christmas

Christmas Lodge

NEWSLETTER

To claim your Two **FREE** Books and find out more about
Rebekah R. Ganiere and her other Upcoming Releases
You can Go Here:
www.RebekahGaniere.com/Newsletter

www.ingramcontent.com/pod-product-compliance
Lightning Source LLC
Chambersburg PA
CBHW030107260626
47156CB00008B/2555